MW01468814

Praise for *Detective Brodie*

"Intriguing, could not put the book down. Great story. Susan really brought the characters to life."

Francis L. Betters

"Loved it, well written. It's hard to find a book that makes you cry, get angry, and laugh all at the same time. This story has it all. I'll be waiting patiently for volume two."

Gloria Dutra

"Amazing, well written, great storyline. This is a book that's hard to put down. It holds your attention. Cannot wait for volume two."

Lynn Maddalena

"Murder, arson, kidnapping—this book has it all without losing its original plot. It's a great story that I recommend to everyone."

Dorothy Iomondi

DETECTIVE BRODIE

DEATH OF A
MILLIONAIRE

DETECTIVE
BRODIE

SUSAN A. BETTERS

TATE PUBLISHING & *Enterprises*

Published by Tate Publishing & Enterprises, LLC
127 E. Trade Center Terrace | Mustang, Oklahoma 73064 USA
1.888.361.9473 | www.tatepublishing.com

Tate Publishing is committed to excellence in the publishing industry. The company reflects the philosophy established by the founders, based on Psalm 68:11,
"The Lord gave the word and great was the company of those who published it."

Book design copyright © 2008 by Tate Publishing, LLC. All rights reserved.
Cover design by Stephanie Woloszyn
Interior design by Janae J. Gass

Published in the United States of America

ISBN: 978-1-60604-592-3
1. Murder, Family Relationships

08.10.14

CHARACTERS

- **Betty Thompson**: a millionaire who died of morphine poisoning. She was in remission from stomach cancer but was getting ready to go for more tests for other stomach problems.

- **Samantha Carlton**: daughter of Betty and mother of Walter and Penny.

- **Walter Carlton**: Samantha's son who had a grudge against his grandmother for having him arrested for drunk driving.

- **Penny Carlton**: Samantha's daughter who gave up cheerleading to help take care of her grandmother.

- **Paul Thompson**: Betty's son and a lawyer.

- **Trisha Thompson**: Paul's wife with a high-class attitude and money to go with it.

- **Cora Thompson**: Paul and Trisha's daughter, head cheerleader, and the most popular girl in school.

- **Candy Thompson**: Paul and Trisha's daughter, a computer whiz, very shy and has few friends in school.

- **Stanley Thompson**: Paul and Trisha's son, a high school football quarterback and the most popular guy in school.

- **William Sander**: gardener who worked for Betty for twenty years and knows all the skeletons in everyone's closet.

- **Harvey Gaunt**: Betty's driver and personal friend whom Betty confided in.

- **Sonia Patterson**: Betty's nurse.

- **Dr. Kendal**: Betty's personal physician in charge of Betty's murder case.

- **Natalie Stone**: Betty's housekeeper.

PROLOGUE

Betty was found dead around one o'clock in the afternoon by her nurse.

There was a family gathering for Betty's sixtieth birthday. Betty went up to her room for a small nap and insisted everyone stay and have fun. Betty had stomach cancer. After many chemotherapy treatments, the cancer was in remission. She was left very weak and still suffered stomach pain. She was scheduled for an ultrasound in three days; in the meantime she was given morphine to help with the pain.

"Everyone is a suspect for one reason or another, and no one leaves until I say so!" said Detective Brodie as he talked with everyone in the family room. Everyone looked around at one another, trying to figure out who had killed Betty.

ONE

Detective Stan Brodie knew when he climbed out of bed it was going to be a long day. He heard his two sons fighting over the television remote, then he heard his wife, Jessica, intervene. He put his jeans on and realized he had trouble buttoning them. At six feet and two hundred pounds, he didn't need to gain any more weight, even though he carried it well. He was all muscle from working out three nights a week at the gym. He looked into the bathroom mirror and ran his hand through his light brown hair. It almost touched his shoulders. Jessica has been trying to get him to cut it, but the stubs he has from not shaving give him a tough look something he needs in his line of work. His blue eye s looked tired and bloodshot. He finished dressing and running a comb through his hair, then put on his holster and gun, hooked his badge to his belt, and went downstairs for coffee.

"Morning, Daddy," Tommy, his youngest son, said as he sat next to his older brother, Brandon, both sulking because they lost television privileges. Tommy is five and looks and acts like Jessica. He has a crew cut and big brown eyes. He is very outgoing, has a good personality, and gets along with everybody. Brandon is more like his father. He's seven; his hair is a tad bit longer then his brother's with blue eyes and sandy brown hair. He's very temperamental.

"Here's your breakfast; eat it while it's hot," Jessica said. "I'm going grocery shopping; is there anything you want, Stan?" Jessica asked as she planted a kiss on his lips. "Yeah, a new brother who doesn't always get his own way," Brandon said as he entered the room.

"Brandon! That is not called for," Jessica snapped. "You were both fighting over the remote, so you both got punished."

"That little nerd started it," Brandon whined.

"I have to go to the station; boys, behave for your mother," Brodie said as he kissed Jessica and ruffled the boys hair before he left.

Brodie stood next to the filing cabinet looking at the missing children's pictures on the wall. It seems that more and more kids go missing every day. The latest one was a twelve-year-old girl. She went to the store for a gallon of milk for her mother and never returned home. Brodie talked to everyone in the neighborhood, but no one saw or heard a thing. He's been trying to track down the mother's ex-boy-friend. It seems he likes little girls way too much.

"Brodie! Come in here," the captain yelled as he opened his office door.

"What's up?" Brodie asked as he sat in a chair across the captain's desk.

"I need you to go to Hampton Avenue to head up the investigation on a suspicious death."

"Come on, captain," Brodie said upset. "I'm working this missing child case; send Dante."

"I need you on this, Brodie," the captain said sternly, "It's Betty Thompson, our benefactor. As you know, she has supported the police force with new uniforms as well as vehicles."

"Her nurse found her dead in her bedroom and the needle of an empty syringe in her arm. I want you over there now and don't talk to the press."

Brodie looked at the big house as he drove up the long driveway. He really didn't have time for another case, but Betty Thompson was a sweet woman. When his house caught fire due to faulty electricity, Betty gave his boys new clothes and shoes and helped him and Jessica get back on their feet. He could not imagine anyone killing such a sweet woman if that was the case.

Brodie walked into Betty's room. She was lying on the bed with the syringe hanging out of her arm. Her room was very neat, so there didn't seem to be a struggle.

"I want everyone's name that was here today," Detective Brodie told the young officer who was standing near the door.

"Everyone is still here, sir. They were having a party for the victim," the officer said.

"Good. Then organize everyone into one room. I want to talk to everybody, and put a few officers at the exits. I don't want anyone leaving until I talk to them."

"Yes, sir," the officer said as he left the room.

"Brodie, are you in charge of this case?" asked Jason, the head of forensics.

"Yeah, what do you have for me?" Brodie asked as he walked around the bed, looking at Betty.

"I want to show you something," Jason said. "Look over

here." He pointed to Betty's wrist. There was purple bruising on both her wrists.

Brodie picked up her arm and looked at the bruising, "She was tied up?" he asked, looking up at Jason.

"No," Jason said, "there are no rope burns or bruising on the other side of her wrist. Look here at these marks." Jason pointed to four long purple marks on Betty's wrist.

"Somebody held her arm, before injecting the morphine," Brodie said, looking at the empty bottle of morphine on the floor.

"If it's morphine," Jason said. "I think you're looking at two people here, not one. Because one person would have to hold her hand while the other injected her with something lethal."

Brodie picked up the empty bottle of morphine from the floor with his pen and placed it in a plastic bag. He rubbed his chin and looked around.

"What's wrong?" Jason asked. "You look a little confused."

"I am." Brodie said. "Her cancer was in remission, so why is she still on morphine, and why is she taking shots instead of pills?"

"She was having stomach problems."

Brodie turned when he heard the voice to see a young woman standing at the door. It was obvious that she has been crying. Her eyes were red and puffy, and she kept sniffling.

"Who are you?" he asked in a demanding voice.

"I'm Sonia Peterson, Betty's nurse. She didn't take the morphine by mouth because of her stomach. She was scheduled for tests in three days."

"What kind of tests?" Brodie asked.

"Ultrasound," Sonia answered. "To see what was causing

her so much pain and to make sure the cancer was still in remission."

"Who found her?" Brodie asked. "And why was she up in her room when the party was for her?"

"She wasn't feeling well. She told everyone to stay and have fun and that she was going to lie down for a little while. I came up thirty minutes later to check on her, and this is how I found her." Sonia cried and then put her hands over her face.

Brodie was not taken in by the crying. He saw too many people cry and scream when a loved one was killed, and it turned out fifty percent of the time that they were the killers. He had to keep his emotions in tack in order to solve this case. "Why did it take you so long to come and check on her?" Brodie asked, a little annoyed.

"I was going to follow her up, but she insisted I stay and have fun," Sonia snapped. "Detective, I love Betty as if she were my own mother If you're insinuating that I had anything to do with her death or neglected her in any way, you are wrong." Sonia snapped and flung her brown wavy hair over her shoulders and glared at Brodie with her big brown eyes and pinched her lips together. She stood five feet six inches and weighed two hundred pounds. She shoved her weight into Brodie as she tried to reach behind him to grab a sweater.

"That stays here," he said as he grabbed the sweater out of her hand. "Nothing leaves this room. And as far as I'm concerned everyone is a suspect, and that means you. If you don't mind going downstairs with the others, I have work to do. I'll be down shortly," Brodie said in a stern voice.

Sonia glared at Brodie then made a huffing noise, turned, and left the room.

"I think she's a little upset with you." Jason said laughing.

"By the time I'm ready to leave here everybody will be mad at me. I'm use to it. It goes along with the job," Brodie said.

"If you're done with the body, I would like to transport it to the morgue. We will know more after the autopsy," Jason said.

"Yeah, I'm done with it. Go ahead and take it. I need to go downstairs, and I hope to get some answers."

Detective Brodie found everyone in the family room; he looked at everyone carefully trying to read their faces. "Everyone is a suspect for one reason or another, and no one leaves until I say so." Detective Brodie said as he talked to everyone in the family room.

Everyone looked around at one another other trying to figure out who would kill Betty.

"Detective, how do you know my mother was murdered?" asked Samantha.

"And you are?" Detective Brodie asked, looking into Samantha's eyes. She had been crying. Her eyes were still a little puffy, but other than that she seemed relatively calm, Detective Brodie thought.

"I'm Samantha Carlton. This is my daughter, Penny," she said as she pointed to a young teenage girl with long sandy blonde hair and big green eyes.

She looked just like her mother. Except for their personal styles, they were identical.

Samantha wore a blue dress that clung to her hips to show off her figure and stopped just above her knees and navy blue pumps. Her hair is light brown, and she wore it loose on her shoulders.

Brodie looked back at Penny. She had on a T-shirt with cutoff jeans that showed off the same figure as her mother's. Her hair was down and tossed about. She also wore a pair of old running shoes with white socks.

"Standing next to the window, Detective, is my son, Walter," Samantha said as she moved to her son's side. He turned and looked at the detective with his hands shoved in the pockets of his beige khaki pants. His white dress shirt hung out over his belt. He wore polished black Dockers, and he had very short blonde hair and green eyes. He kept his lips pinched together and his eyes showed a lot of remorse. Detective Brodie stood staring at him. For a moment he saw real pain and remorse. *Was it from guilt or real sadness?* he wondered.

"One by one I want the rest of your names," he said as he looked at everyone else in the room. "Starting with you," he said to a very nervous man standing near the fireplace.

"I'm Paul Thompson, Betty's son. This is my wife," he said as he put his arm around a very stylish lady who had on more jewelry then he ever saw one woman wear.

She wore a very expensive sequin gown with a pearl necklace around her neck. She wore her dark brown hair in a French braid with diamond pins all around it. Her gown clung to her body, showing every curve of her figure. Her nails were well-manicured, painted red with little diamonds in the middle. Even her toes were painted, Detective Brodie noticed when he looked down at her three-inch pumps. Her brown eyes showed no sadness or remorse. *She can't wait to get her hands on Betty's money*, he thought.

"What's your first name, Mrs. Thompson?" Detective Brodie asked.

"Trisha. Would you like me to spell it for you?" she said with the words rolling softly off her lips.

"I do know how to spell." Detective Brodie said, annoyed trying not to let this lady get under his skin with her high-class attitude.

"What are the kids' names?" he asked Paul, who was leaning against the fireplace with one arm on the marble mantel and the other holding a drink.

Detective Brodie watched him as he took a long gulp of his drink, spilling a little on his white dress shirt. He stood six feet tall and had sandy brown hair and green eyes like his sister. He was so well-built you could see the muscles through his shirt. His sleeves wore rolled up halfway, and his shirt hung out of his black dress pants. He had a lost look in his eyes, or maybe it was from too much alcohol.

"Those are my daughters, Candy and Cora, and my son, Stanley, is over there."

Detective Brodie was looking at the appearance in both girls, Cora was very stylish, like her mother, with long brown hair and a red dress that was a little too short. It had a V-neck, and she wore a pearl necklace. Her fingernails were painted red. She wore four-inch pumps. She was very thin. She had no remorse or tears in her eyes.

Candy stood in the corner sobbing. She was definitely different. She had brown shoulder-length hair, glasses with gold rims and small frames, and she wore overalls and a black T-shirt with running shoes that showed a lot of wear and tear.

Detective Brodie studied Candy for a moment. She really seemed to be taking Betty's death hard, and she sobbed the entire time without stopping. He then looked over at Stanley. He was a big boy: he stood about six feet tall like his dad, had to be at least two hundred pounds, with most of it muscle, like his father, and he had big beefy hands. He wore a football jersey. Detective Brodie remembered seeing him play. He's the high school quarterback, the star player. Stanley stood watching him, making Detective Brodie uncomfortable. He turned his attention to the driver.

"And your name is?" he asked Betty's driver.

"Harvey Gaunt. I'm Betty's driver and friend," he answered in a somber voice.

Brodie could tell he was extremely upset. His voice cracked when he talked as he tried to hold back tears. He stood five feet five inches tall and was very skinny with a long face and pale blue eyes. His hair was very thin and had a lot of balding spots. Brodie figured he had to be in his late sixties to early seventies.

Brodie turned and looked at another man sitting in a chair with his face in his hands, sobbing quietly. "What's your name and what do you do here?"

"I'm William Sanders," he said looking up at Brodie. "I'm the gardener. For twenty years I worked for Betty," he said between sobs and put his face in his hands.

Brodie stood watching the man's demeanor for a few seconds. He was very distraught and sobbed openly. He was very thin with long shaky fingers and gray hair that was in need of a comb, pale skin, and deep-set brown eyes. Brodie had a feeling this man's feelings were genuine.

"I'm Dr. Kendal, Betty's personal physician and friend," the doctor said as he entered the room.

Brodie turned around and came face to face with a big man about six feet and at least three hundred pounds, with thick wavy brown hair, big brown eyes, and a trimmed mustache and beard.

"Do you mind answering some questions for me, doctor?" Brodie asked.

"Of course not, Detective. I'll help any way I can," the doctor answered.

"What was the morphine prescribed for, and what was her usual dosage?" Brodie asked, taking out his notepad and pen.

"She was having a lot of trouble with her stomach. She couldn't eat. She was in constant pain. Her nurse would give her a shot as needed for pain. She was scheduled for tests in three days."

"If she was in that much pain, why wasn't she in the hospital?" Brodie asked, looking confused.

"Betty wanted to wait until after her party. I believe she felt her cancer was out of remission and spreading, and she wanted to have one last time with her whole family," the doctor explained.

"And what do you think?" Brodie asked.

"I believe the cancer came back and spread. That's why I ordered the morphine shots, to make her as comfortable as possible. She knew if it came back that she would only have about three to six months to live."

Everyone in the room gasped when they heard the doctor.

Brodie looked at everyone and then continued, "I guess that was too long for someone to wait," Brodie said with a hint of disgust.

"Detective," Paul said as he stood. "None of us knew her cancer was back."

"I don't believe none of you had any idea her cancer was back with all the pain she was in," Brodie said.

Nobody said a word they all sat with their heads down looking at the floor.

"I need everybody's whereabouts from the time Betty went upstairs until she was found. Starting with you," he said, pointing to Betty's daughter, Samantha.

Samantha looked up, mystified. "Do you think I would kill my mother?" Samantha asked in an angry voice.

"Ma'am, right now I have a dead woman and a house full of people. As I said before, everybody in this room is a suspect. If you don't mind answering my question, I would like to wrap this up so I can investigate your mother's death."

Samantha put her hands on her hips. "I was in the garden picking some fresh flowers for my mother's room."

"Was anybody with you? Or did anyone see you in the garden?" Brodie asked as he wrote in his notepad.

"I was alone, and I don't know if anyone saw me. There are a lot of people here. You will have to ask them and find out," Samantha said, annoyed that she was being questioned in her mother's death.

Brodie wrote in his notepad, "Did anyone see Mrs. Carlton in the garden"? he asked, looking around the room.

"I did," Penny said, coming to her mother's defense.

"What time was that?" Brodie asked, a little doubtful that she actually saw her mother.

"It was right after my grandmother went up to rest. I wanted to go home, so I went looking for my mother. I saw her in the garden."

"You didn't talk to your mother, did you"? Brodie asked with more doubt.

"No, I was about to when my cousin Candy called me, so I went to see what she wanted."

Detective Brodie looked around the room, "Where is Candy?" he asked.

"Right here, Detective. I had to go to the bathroom," Candy answered in a shy voice.

"Did you hear what your cousin Penny had to say?" he asked.

"No," Candy answered, looking confused as she looked at Penny.

"Good. Let's go into the other room and talk," Brodie said as he led Candy to the door, then stopped and turned to everyone else in the room. "Nobody is to leave this room until I say so." He then closed the door and took Candy across the hall to the sitting room.

"Sit down and make yourself comfortable," Brodie said. "I have a few questions."

"Okay," Candy answered nervously. She sat on the wing chair and folded her hands in her lap.

"What were you doing when your grandmother went upstairs to lie down?" Brodie asked.

Tears came to Candy's eyes, thinking of her grandmother. "I was helping Natalie clean up."

"Natalie," Brodie said, confused. "Who is she?"

"She's grandmother's housekeeper. Nobody was helping her clean, and there was a huge mess, so I decided to help her clean."

"That's very nice of you," Brodie said sincerely. "What about Penny? Did you see her at all?"

"Yes. Just before the nurse started screaming, I called Penny to see if she wanted to go for a walk down by the stream," Candy answered.

"It was just before the nurse screamed?" Brodie asked, tapping his pen on the pad.

"Where did Penny come from?"

"Around the back of the house. I didn't have a chance to talk to her. The nurse screamed, and we all went running to where she was."

"Did you see Mrs. Carlton at all?"

"Yes. Aunt Samantha came running from the side of the house."

Brodie wrote in his notepad, "Was anyone that you could think of mad at your grandmother? Even if it's something small that you may not think is important."

Candy put her head down, and she shook her head yes. "Walter was very angry at grandmother for having him arrested for drunk driving," her lips quivered. "But I know Walter; he could never hurt anyone."

"When and how did this come about your grandmother having him arrested?"

Brodie asked with total concern.

"Last night," Candy answered. "He was supposed to mow grandmother's lawn. Instead, he sat by the creek drinking with his buddies. William, grandmother's gardener caught him. He chased Walter's friends away and hauled Walter off to grandmother. She threatened to call his mother and have her come down. Walter got mad and started to leave, and grandmother told him he was too drunk to drive and if he left she would call the police because she didn't want anybody's blood on her hands. Walter snickered and left, not believing that grandmother would have him arrested."

"How do you know all this?" Brodie asked.

"Aunt Samantha called my dad to bail him out of jail. When Dad came home, he was angry. Walter had a bad attitude, and Aunt Samantha should have left him in jail."

"Thank you, Candy. You have been a lot of help," Brodie said as he stood up. "Ask your father to come in here, please."

"Detective, you won't tell Walter what I said, will you?" Candy asked worriedly.

"No, it's between us. The police records I'll get from the station later." After Candy left, Brodie waited for Paul.

"Detective, you wanted to talk to me?" Paul Thompson asked as he entered the room.

"Take a seat, Mr. Thompson. I have a few questions for you."

Paul sat in the same wing chair that Penny sat in. He crossed his legs and put his arms on the armrest.

"Where were you when your mother went upstairs to take a nap?" Brodie asked as he looked at his notes.

Paul put his head down. "I was tossing the football with

my son for a while, and then I went to sit in the gazebo to have a smoke and glass of wine."

"Did anybody see you in the gazebo?"

Paul thought for a minute. "Yeah, the gardener came by and waved."

"Why did you sit in the gazebo by yourself? And why did you not have your wife sit with you? A gazebo by the lake and wine is very romantic," Brodie said.

Paul chuckled. "My wife hates the smell of cigarettes and the bugs at the water. Romance to her is a five-star hotel and a five-hundred-dollar bottle of champagne," Paul said sarcastically.

"Your wife is high maintenance?" Brodie asked.

"You could say that," Paul answered. "She likes to try to keep up with the Jones, if you know what I mean."

"Yes, I do," Brodie said, not that his wife was like that. She was the total opposite. If she couldn't get it on sale, she didn't want it. She also loved to shop in thrift shops.

Paul cleared his throat, taking Brodie out of his thoughts. "Do you know anyone that has a grudge or is angry with your mother in any way?"

"Yeah, my punk nephew, Walter." Paul told him the same story Candy had told him about Walter's arrest. "I should have left him in jail for the night."

"What happened at the police station that would want you to leave your nephew in jail?" Brodie asked.

"I bailed him out. We went into the holding room to get his things, and he started griping about his grandmother. Samantha yelled at him. He turned and pushed his mother and glared at her as if he wanted to hit her. I grabbed his arm and told him I would break his arm if he ever put another hand on his mother. He smirked, let out a small laugh, and strutted out of the station like he was king."

Brodie rubbed his chin, and wrote more in his notepad. "Do you think he is capable of murder?" Brodie asked.

"A few months ago I would have said no, but now I don't know," Paul said, putting his head down.

"What changed?" Brodie asked.

"His father up and left his mother with the next-door neighbor. Apparently they had been having an affair for six months. Walter and his father were buddies, and when his father left Walter couldn't forgive him. He became mean, hanging with the wrong kids, and smoking pot. He turned into a boy I don't know anymore."

"Thank you, Mr. Thompson. Could you please send your wife in?" Brodie said as he shook Paul's hand.

Brodie sat looking at his notepad; all he had were a lot of unanswered questions. "Could Walter really be that angry at his grandmother that he would kill her?"

Paul walked into the family room, shoulders slumped as he sat in the nearest chair. "He wants to talk to you," he said to his wife, Trisha.

"What's going on, Paul?" Trisha asked.

"He wants to talk to you that's what's going on," Paul said, annoyed.

Paul looked around the room. Cora, his oldest daughter, looked bored. *Just like her mother,* he thought. *Unless it's for her benefit, she doesn't want anything to do with it.* His son, Stanley, stood next to the window talking to Walter in a whisper. He then turned to Candy, his baby girl. She looked up and caught her father's eyes and went to sit on his lap. Candy always makes him feel good; she is down to earth and so loving. It's a shame nobody can see all her good qualities. She has no real friends, and her own sister makes her feel like an outcast. Paul hugged his daughter tighter as she put her head on his shoulder.

Brodie looked up at Trisha as she walked into the room. Her lips were squeezed tight, and her eyes showed a hint of annoyance. "Sit down, Mrs. Thompson," Brodie instructed.

He watched her as she sat in the wing chair and crossed her legs and then smoothed her dress with her hands as though she was trying to take out invisible wrinkles. "Where were you when your mother-in law went upstairs to take a nap?"

Trisha patted the top of her hair to make sure every piece was still in place. "I was sitting in the sunroom drinking ice tea with Cora."

"Were you there the whole time?" Brodie asked as he wrote in his notepad.

"Yes, Detective, I was, up until I heard that nurse's frightful scream."

"Do you know anyone that would want to murder your mother -in law?"

"No, I don't. Everybody loved Betty," Trisha said with strained remorse.

"No, everybody didn't love Betty, or I wouldn't be here," Brodie said with a stern voice. "What about your nephew, Walter? I heard he was very upset with his grandmother."

Trisha let out a forced laugh. "Walter is angry with everybody, but he's not capable of murder."

"And what makes you say that?" Brodie asked as he looked into Trisha's eyes.

"Detective, if you knew Walter as I do, you would understand that he's just a lost boy," Trisha said with genuine concern in her voice.

Brodie tapped his pen on the notepad and then looked at Trisha. "Make me understand," Brodie said tiredly.

"I'm sorry; I can't tell you too much. Walter trusts me, and we talk a lot," Trisha said not looking at Brodie.

"Listen!" Brodie snapped. "This is a murder investigation, and Walter is my only suspect right now, so tell me everything you know or I will charge Walter with murder." He was trying to bluff Trisha, hoping it worked, because the truth was he had a room full of suspects.

"Okay, I'll tell you everything," Trisha said, annoyed. "Walter comes over to talk to me a lot because I'm the only one who understands him. You see my father also ran out on my mother when I was Walter's age. Walter is learning to deal with it, but he has a lot of pressure on him right know."

"What kind of pressure?" Brodie asked as he sat back in the chair listening to Trisha's story.

"For one, my husband. He's been on Walter's case about joining the football team and to become an athlete like Stanley, but Walter isn't into sports. He loves working on cars. Paul gets upset when he sees Walter working on a car, telling him he's going to grow up to be a nobody and that if he wants to get ahead in this world he needs to get an athletic scholarship."

"There's nothing wrong with wanting what's best for

your nephew," Brodie said, trying to figure out where this story was going.

Trisha looked at Brodie with a stern look. "What about what Walter wants?" Trisha said in a stern voice. "He loves to work on cars. He has good grades. Yes, he's hanging with the wrong kids that like to drink. He's a sixteen-year-old boy who is confused and under pressure, but he loves his grandmother and is very remorseful about what he did. He knows his grandmother only has his best interest at heart."

Brodie rubbed his chin. "Is there anything else you would like to tell me before we finish up?" he asked.

"No, Detective, that's it. When you talk to Walter, you will see the scared boy I see," Trisha said with sadness in her voice.

"I will be looking forward to talking with him," Brodie said as he stood up. "Send Cora in please." Brodie waited until Trisha left the room before he let out a big groan. Walter was his best suspect, but if what Trisha said was true, he needed to rethink this case.

Cora walked in, looking like she didn't have a care in the world. She plopped down in the chair. "What's up?" she said as she smiled at Brodie.

Brodie was taken aback by her demeanor. Her grandmother had been murdered, and she was acting like she's at some friend's house catching up on the latest gossip.

"Where were you when your grandmother went upstairs to take a nap?" Brodie asked sternly, not caring for this young girl sitting in front of him.

"I was in the sun room having ice tea with my mother," Cora answered with a smile still plastered on her face.

"The whole time?" Brodie asked with a hint of disgust at this girl's attitude.

"For about fifteen minutes. Then I went to call my boyfriend."

"You were only with your mother for fifteen minutes?" Brodie asked, confused.

"Yeah. I know it was fifteen minutes because I was waiting to call my boyfriend. He gets off work around one thirty, and I had to wait fifteen minutes for him to get home," Cora said, twirling her hair around her fingers.

"How long were you on the phone for?" Brodie asked as he wrote in his notepad, "before you heard the nurse's screams?"

"I wasn't. My boyfriend wasn't home, so I just sat by the phone calling every few minutes. I never did get in touch with him," Cora said.

She sounded more annoyed that her boyfriend wasn't home than that her grandmother was murdered.

"What did you do when you heard the screams?" Brodie asked sternly.

"Nothing," Cora replied.

Brodie looked at her astonished. "You heard your grandmother's nurse scream, and you did nothing?" he asked, shocked.

"I didn't think it was serious. I thought she saw a mouse or something," Cora said, rolling her eyes.

"Did anyone see you on the phone or sitting there the whole time?" Brodie asked, getting more annoyed with her.

"No, nobody," she answered casually.

"When did you realize something was wrong?" Brodie asked.

"I heard someone yell that grandmother was dead. That's when I ran to grandmother's room. She was just lying there not moving," Cora said in amazement.

"That's normally what dead people do just lay there and don't move," Brodie said sarcastically, wanting to end this interview because Cora Thompson was getting under his skin. "Send in your brother please."

"But don't you want to know whom I think could have killed grandmother?" Cora asked, looking at Brodie with eagerness in her eyes to blame someone.

"No, it's my job to figure it out." If it were anybody else, Brodie would have welcomed their opinion. He did not want to get this girl started on a ludicrous story.

Cora pouted as she left the room to go get her brother.

"I hope her brother has more sense than she does," Brodie muttered to himself.

"Detective, you want to see me?" Stanley Thompson said as he entered the room.

Brodie looked him over. He had sad eyes and a stern look on his face. His eyes were a little puffy from crying. *At least this young man has feelings*, Brodie thought as he took a seat across from Stanley.

"Could you tell me where you were when your grandmother went upstairs to take a nap?"

"I was tossing the football around with my dad for a bit, and then I went for a walk with my cousin Walter around the grounds."

"What kind of conversation did you and Walter have?" Brodie asked.

"Walter was upset that grandmother called the cops on him and having him arrested. He was also angry with my dad for treating him the way he did at the station," Stanley said and then stopped and looked at Brodie as though he had said a little too much.

"Do you think Walter is capable of murder?" Brodie asked, looking into Stanley's eyes and seeing total shock.

"No way, man. Walter was angry, but he knew grandmother was only trying to stop him from killing himself or someone else."

"What did your father do at the police station that made Walter so upset?" Brodie asked as he looked at his notes.

"When Walter came into the holding room, my dad shoved Walter into the wall, put his fist in Walter's face, and told him the next time he did something that stupid he would break his nose, and then he punched Walter in the shoulder."

"What did Walter do when your father threatened him?" Brodie asked with concern.

"He just snickered and walked out of the room. That's Walter's way of dealing with things."

"And what way is that?" Brodie asked.

Stanley sat straight up and ran his big beefy hands through his hair. "He snickers. He won't let you know you got the best of him."

"Could you think of anyone that would want to harm your grandmother?" Brodie asked, looking into Stanley's eyes.

Stanley looked down at the floor and shook his head no. When he lifted his head, up there were tears coming down his face.

"Thank you, Stanley" Brodie said as he stood up. "Could you please send Walter in?"

"Detective, please find the person who did this to my grandmother," Stanley said as he shook Brodie's hand.

Brodie was moved because he was the only person to make that statement. "I promise you I will," Brodie answered.

Walter came into the room looking like he just lost his best friend. His eyes were drawn. His lips were pinched, and walked with his head down and his back hunched.

"Please, Walter, sit down," Brodie said as Walter walked into the room. "Can you tell me where you were when your grandmother went up for a nap?"

Walter rubbed the sweat beads that were forming on his head. "I watched my uncle and cousin Stanley toss the football, and then me and Stanley went for a walk."

"Walter, I have been getting some disturbing stories about your temper. Would you care to tell me about it?"

"I bet you heard a lot of bad stuff," Walter said with a snicker.

"Yes, I have, but I want to hear your side," Brodie said, looking directly at Walter. He watched Walter's actions as he shifted in the chair. He seemed very uncomfortable. When Walter looked at Brodie, he noticed obvious pain in the boy's eyes.

"I got into some trouble and was hauled off to jail," Walter said, trying to sound casual.

"Would you care to elaborate?" Brodie asked.

"My grandmother called the cops on me for drinking and driving. I got picked up, and Uncle Paul came and bailed me out."

"You were pretty upset with your grandmother for having you arrested," Brodie said, trying to get some reaction out of Walter.

"Yeah, I was," Walter snapped, but then he spoke softly. Brodie had to strain to hear what Walter was saying. "When I woke up this morning, I knew I had to apologize to my grandmother. She called the cops because she loves me and didn't want to see me hurt," Walter said.

"Did you apologize to your grandmother?" Brodie asked, not sure how to react to this boy's emotions. Part of him wanted to believe that he was forcing remorse, but he felt his emotions were genuine.

"I went there before everyone else so I would have time alone to talk to her. She was lying down upstairs. Her nurse didn't want me to bother her, but I went up anyway. I apologized, and she gave me a hug and kiss. And I promised her I would never drink and drive again. I have to keep that promise," Walter said, putting his head down. "I want to make her proud."

"I'm sure she is very proud of you. It takes a real man to apologize and admit when he is wrong. Did you talk about anything else?" Brodie asked, feeling real remorse for this kid.

"We talked about my uncle Paul," Walter said, looking down at his hands.

"What about your uncle Paul?" Brodie asked curiously.

"Uncle Paul was really upset when he bailed me out. He slammed me into the wall and threatened to break my nose. He called my grandmother and told her I was mouthy and showed no appreciation for him bailing me out. I told my grandmother the truth."

"What did your grandmother say about the way your uncle treated you?"

"She was really upset. She said uncle Paul had a temper as long as she could remember. When he was a teenager, she put him in counseling. She said he refused to go and my grandfather always gave into him," Walter said, looking a little teary eyed.

"Do you know if she said anything to your uncle about the way he treated you at the station?" Brodie asked with great concern.

"Yeah, she called him up and started yelling at him. I don't know what he said, but it made grandmother very angry. Her face turned red, and she told him to stay out of her life and not to come over today. He came anyway, and grandmother was not too happy."

"How do you know she wasn't happy?" Brodie asked, getting excited with this new information.

"She didn't say anything. She just glared at him, and when Uncle Paul went over to give grandmother a kiss on the cheek, she pulled away and turned her back on him."

"Did anyone else see this?" Brodie asked

"Everyone did. We were all standing there, but no one said anything because they all know how Uncle Paul is. They probably figured he and grandmother were arguing again," Walter said, rubbing his eyes and letting out a yawn.

"I'm sorry. I know you had a rough night," Brodie said. "But I just have a few more questions. "Why did your grandmother and uncle argue all the time?"

"I really don't know. You know how it goes the kids are always left in the dark," Walter said with a smirk.

Brodie couldn't help but laugh. "You never heard them argue then?" Brodie asked.

"Everybody heard them arguing. And that's when us kids were pushed out the door. We never heard anything except Uncle Paul yelling about grandmother not caring. We had no clue as to what he was talking about," Walter said between yawns.

"Thank you, Walter; you have been a big help," Brodie said as he stood up and extended his hand to Walter.

"Detective, when you find the person who killed my grandmother, shoot him," Walter said in a stern voice.

Brodie patted Walter on the back. "I can't shoot the person, but I will put that person behind bars for a very long time."

Brodie followed Walter into the family room. Everyone turned and looked with curious looks on their faces. "Everyone is free to leave, but before you do I want you all to put your phone number and address on this paper," Brodie said as he laid the paper and pen on the table. "And no one is to leave town until I'm done with this investigation. I want all the employees to stay put."

One by one they put their phone number and address on the paper and left.

When there was nobody left but the employees, Brodie turned to them, "I want to talk to all of you in private, and I'll start with you," Brodie said, pointing to the nurse.

Brodie sat in the same chair in the sitting room that he had sat in when he interviewed all the family members.

"Your name is Sonia Peterson?" Brodie asked as he looked at his notepad.

"Yes, I'm Betty's nurse." Sonia stopped talking and rubbed the tears that were starting to form in her eyes. "I'm sorry, I was Betty's nurse."

"Did you always call her Betty?" Brodie asked.

"Yes, she hated to be called Mrs. Thompson. She insisted that we all call her Betty," Sonia said, trying to maneuver her big body into the wing chair to get comfortable and then gave up and moved across the room to the sofa.

Brodie had to move to the sofa as well so he could hear Sonia when she spoke.

"How long have you been Betty's nurse?" Brodie asked once he was settled on the sofa.

"Six years," Sonia said with tears welling up in her eyes again. "That's when she was first diagnosed with cancer."

"How would you describe your relationship with Betty?" Brodie asked, looking up at Sonia.

"It was great. She was the mother I never really had." And then Sonia started to weep.

"I know this is hard, and I'm sorry," Brodie said. "But I need to ask you a few more questions.

Sonia blew her nose and shook her head yes. "I know, Detective, and I want to help you any way I can."

"I appreciate that," Brodie said. He wrote in his notepad. "How well did Betty's children get along with her?"

"Betty and Samantha got along great. Samantha was always coming over or calling when she couldn't make it just to check on Betty. She always bought Betty little gifts."

"What kind of gifts?" Brodie asked, not sure if it was

important or not, but he didn't want to leave any stones unturned.

"Little figurines of angels those were Betty's favorite. Or she would bring flowers or chocolate, little things to let her mother know she was thinking of her."

"How did Paul get along with Betty?" Brodie asked, hoping to get the answer he wanted.

Sonia's eyes turned stormy, and her lips quivered. "Paul is no good. He only came by for money, not to see his mother."

Brodie was writing in the notepad. "Did Betty give him money all the time?" Brodie asked, looking at Sonia's angry demeanor as she tapped her fingers on the couch and rocked her foot. She pinched her lips together before she spoke.

"No. Betty got tired of him only coming over for money. She warned him that if he didn't budget his money more carefully he would be in the poor house and she would not bail him out."

"Was that because his wife is high maintenance?" Brodie asked. "Is that where all the money went to?"

Sonia's eyes got big, and then she laughed. "Trisha is far from high maintenance. She hates dressing the way she does and wearing all that jewelry," Sonia laughed. "She wears all that stuff because Paul demands that she fit the image of his law buddies' wives. Trisha would rather wear a T-shirt and jeans. The money goes to his high-class lifestyle."

Brodie looked a little confused. "What do you mean his high-class lifestyle?"

Brodie asked, rubbing the back of his neck.

"He makes close to fifty thousand dollars a year. I know because Betty is always yelling at him about it, and he spends seventy to seventy-five thousand dollars a year. He takes his law buddies out for lobster dinners. He bought a boat because one of his buddies bought one. He drives a Porsche and bought Trisha a Lexus, which she didn't want. She was happy driving her Caravan."

Brodie rubbed his neck again. "What happened when Betty stopped giving him money?"

"He was furious. He had to sell his boat, and he yelled at Betty for three days about it, telling her 'he was the laughing stock of the firm.' He said he didn't want people to think he couldn't afford the finer things in life. Betty simply told him that he could have a nice life if he budgeted his money, which made him angry. He turned red and told her she was cheap and only cared about was herself."

"Do you know how he is making ends meet now?" Brodie asked.

"He sold Trisha's Lexus, but insisted she wear all her jewelry and dress like she is going to a ball so everyone won't think they're broke," Sonia said.

"His image is important to him, more than his family, I take it," Brodie said mainly to himself as he wrote in his notepad.

"Yes, sir, it is. He tries to impose it on his children. Cora is easy. She loves to dress up and chase the boys, but Candy is different. She wears what she wants and doesn't care how anybody sees her."

"How dose Paul feel about that? Not so good, I bet," Brodie said with a hint of humor.

"That's what puzzles me," Sonia said. "Candy can dress the way she wants, and it doesn't bother Paul one bit. He's always calling Candy his baby girl as though he is more proud of her than his other two children, even though he brags about Stanley being the school star quarterback."

"Thank you, Sonia. You have been a great help." Brodie questioned the rest of the staff and heard the same story about Paul wasting money and fighting with Betty over it. Brodie didn't want to jump to conclusions yet. He didn't want any mistakes. He walked around Betty's room, looking at all her angels that Samantha bought her. He then went to the bed. He stood looking at it for a while. Just as he was getting ready to leave, he noticed something sticking out of the mattress. He bent down and pulled out Betty's journal. He opened it slowly to make sure there was nothing inside that might fall out. He glanced through the pages and then closed the journal and headed down the stairs to go home.

"Excuse me, Detective."

Detective Brodie stopped and turned around. It was Betty's driver, Harvey Gaunt.

"Is that Betty's journal?" he asked, concerned and pointing to the book under Brodie's arm.

"Yes, it is," Brodie answered. "How did you know Betty kept a journal? And more importantly, why didn't you tell me?"

"I'm sorry, Detective, but before you read that we need to talk," Harvey said, extremely nervous.

Brodie looked confused. "Okay, talk," Brodie said.

"In private," Harvey said as he started walking to the sitting room.

Brodie followed. *What could be in this journal that has this man so nervous,* Brodie thought to himself.

Once they were in the sitting room, Brodie sat on the

sofa while Harvey looked out the big picture window. He then cleared his throat and turned and looked at Brodie and then back to the window.

"What's going on?" Brodie asked. "What's in this journal that got you so upset?"

Harvey spoke without turning around, and he continued to look out the window. "Betty and I were lovers," he said in a soft voice. "Betty didn't want her kids to know because it started while she was still married to Charlie. He never loved her, and Betty knew it. She believed he did for the longest time, and maybe he did for a bit. But once the children were born he changed. He drank a lot and was never home." Harvey stopped for a second and turned to Brodie. "Betty always talked to me about him. She trusted me and confided in me. One thing led to another, and we became lovers. I wanted Bett y to divorce him and marry me, but she wouldn't. Her kids needed their father she would say, so we just continued our affair."

Brodie sat stunned as Harvey talked. "When Charlie died why didn't you get together? Brodie asked.

"Believe me, I wanted to," Harvey said. "But Betty said it was too soon and that the children would never accept it, and then she found out she had cancer."

"What stopped her then?" Brodie asked. "Was it fear of putting you through her illness?"

"No," Harvey said. "It was fear of dying and her kids thinking badly of her. She wanted her kids respect when she died, and she believed if she told them about us she would lose their respect."

"So you continued being lovers?" Brodie asked.

Susan A. Betters

"No, Betty wanted to end it. She said she loved me but she had to get her affairs in order and she was afraid of being caught because Samantha started showing up unannounced to check on Betty."

"Wow," Brodie said. "It must have been tough on you."

"What is tough on me is knowing I am never going to see that sweet face again." Harvey collapsed on the couch and cried into his hands.

Brodie, not knowing what to make of all this, patted Harvey on the back and consoled him.

T W O

Dinner was on the table when he walked into his house. The boys were not around, because if they were they would have immediately attacked him when he came through the door.

"Where are the boys?" Brodie asked in a tired voice.

"I sent them next door," Jessica said as she kissed Brodie on the lips. "Honey, I am so sorry," she said in a sad voice. "I heard what happened to Betty Thompson." Jessica put her head down and moaned. "I can't believe somebody would kill that sweet woman."

"I know, baby," Brodie said as he put his arms around Jessica. He smelled her shampoo as she put her head on his shoulder.

"What happened, Stan?" Jessica asked.

"I believe it was morphine poisoning, but I won't know for sure until I get the toxicology test back," Brodie said as he sat down at the kitchen table.

"What makes you think morphine?" Jessica asked.

"There was an empty morphine bottle on the floor and a syringe hanging out of her arm," Brodie said, pushing his dinner around with his fork.

"Do you have any suspects?" Jessica asked softly.

"Just when I think I do, another snag comes up. A lot of

suspects and no evidence," Brodie said tiredly. "I'm not really hungry," he said as he pushed his dinner away and grabbed a beer from the refrigerator.

Jessica cleaned the table and then joined Brodie on the couch. She snuggled in his arms and ran her hand over his chest.

Brodie moaned at Jessica's touch. He took her hand in his and kissed it.

Jessica tilted her head up and then kissed his lips.

"Mommy, we're here," the boys yelled as they ran into the house and jumped into Brodie's lap. "Hi, Daddy," they both said in unison.

Brodie played on the floor with the boys until their bath time, and then he helped tuck them into bed and kissed them each on the head.

"I love you, Dad," Brandon said from the top bunk. "I love you too, Daddy," came Tommy's voice from the bottom bunk.

"I love you both. No fooling around, go right to sleep," Brodie said as he shut off the bedroom light.

When he got comfortable on the living room sofa, he pulled out Betty's journal.

"What's that?" Jessica asked as she snuggled close to him on the couch.

"It's Betty's journal," Brodie answered. "I found it under her bed." He started flipping through the pages. "Listen, baby, I'm going to be up for a while reading this journal. Why don't you go to bed. "I'll be up as soon as I can."

"All right," Jessica said as she gave Brodie a kiss. "I love you. Don't stay up too long." She rubbed his shoulder and then headed up to bed.

"I love you too," Brodie yelled back and then opened the journal and started reading.

The first few pages were about her affair with Harvey. That's about the time she started keeping the journal. After twenty minutes of reading, Brodie came across an interesting page. He read it twice to make sure he read it right.

> I don't want to believe such evil thoughts about my own son, but there is something unnatural about his relationship with his daughter Candy. I don't know what it is. I tried talking with Candy, but she got very defensive about her father. I don't know what to do. I hope and pray I'm wrong.

Brodie rubbed his chin and then went back to his conversation with Candy. She was definitely different from the rest of the family. She was shy and withdrawn but very eager to talk about Walter. Paul was also eager to blame Walter. Maybe Walter knew something, and they were trying to get him out of the way. Brodie knew he was jumping to conclusions. But there was something that worried Betty about her son and granddaughter's relationship. Brodie yawned and rubbed his eyes. He laid the journal on his chest for a few minutes and closed his eyes. Before long he was fast asleep.

Jessica rolled over to put her arm around Brodie and felt his side of the bed empty.

She knew he never got up before her. She found him sleeping soundly on the couch. She put the coffee on, knowing she had a few minutes to herself before the boys got up.

She took the journal off Brodie's chest and laid it on the table. She then went and started breakfast.

Brodie smelled the coffee and opened his eyes. He spotted Jessica frying eggs and trying to make toast at the same time. He walked behind her and put his arms around her waist and kissed her neck. "Mmm, you smell good," he moaned in her ear. She turned with a big smile on her face and planted a big kiss on his lips. He pulled her into him and started stroking her back, running his hands up through her hair as he kissed her lips and then her neck.

Jessica felt Brodie's arousal and pushed him back. "Go take a cold shower," she said, laughing. "The boys will be down any minute."

Brodie moaned and poured himself a cup of coffee. "What happened to us? We use to be all over each other," Brodie asked with a smile.

"We had children," Jessica said as she put her hand on Brodie's chest and gave him another kiss. But before Brodie could respond, they heard the boys racing down the stairs.

They all ate a peaceful breakfast without the boys arguing.

"Come on, boys, time to get dressed for school. And then you can watch fifteen minutes of cartoons if you don't fight," Jessica said.

Brodie watched the boys scramble upstairs to get dressed as he poured himself another coffee and ate his toast. "I need to get to the station. I'll call you if I'm going to be late tonight. Boys, I'm leaving," he yelled up the stairs. "Be good for your mother."

"Bye, Daddy," both boys yelled.

Jessica walked Brodie to the door and kissed him. Just as he was about to leave, Brandon came running down the stairs.

"I love you, Dad," Brandon said as he gave Brodie a hug.

"I love you too, son," Brodie said as he hugged Brandon and then kissed the top of his head.

Brodie sat at his desk going over his notes from his interview with the family members. He was a little taken back because they all lied except Walter and Stanley. Samantha said she was picking flowers for her mother's room, but there were no cut flowers anywhere. There should have been some on the ground that she would have dropped when she heard the nurse screaming. And then Penny she said she saw her mother in the garden just after Betty went upstairs and then heard Candy call her so she went to see her cousin instead. Candy contradicted her story, stating she called Penny just before the nurse screamed. That means it had to be at least thirty minutes or so after her grandmother went upstairs and that she saw Penny coming from the back of the house and her aunt Samantha coming from the side. The garden is in the front, so neither one could have been in the garden. Paul said he was smoking a cigarette in the gazebo and drinking a glass of wine. When Brodie inspected it, the seats were just painted and still damp. William, the gardener, stated he had just got done painting it and was going to put fresh flowers all around it for Betty because she loved to sit out there at night and watch the stars. He also stated that no one ever sits in the gazebo, so he knew it wouldn't be a problem painting it. He wanted it all set for that night for Betty. It was her birthday present from him.

Trisha stated that she was in the sunroom with Cora the whole time drinking ice tea, but Cora said she was only with her mother for fifteen minutes before she left to call her boyfriend. Why would they all lie? What were they hiding? Brodie knew he had to interview them all again, but first he wanted to go back to Betty's and check things out again. Just as Brodie was getting ready to leave, his phone rang. He moaned. "This is Brodie," he said as he picked up the phone.

"Brodie, it's Jason. I have some news for you. Mrs. Thompson had a lethal dose of morphine in her system."

"So she died of morphine poisoning," Brodie said, having already known.

"That's not all," Jason said

"What do you mean?" Brodie asked.

"The morphine was a cover up to make it look like she killed herself. She also had high doses of rat poison in her stomach. There was also no sign of cancer. It was still in remission," Jason stated.

"What are you telling me the rat poison killed her?" Brodie asked, confused.

"That's exactly what killed her," Jason stated.

"If her cancer was still in remission, what caused her stomach pain?" Brodie asked, more confused.

"It was the rat poisoning. She was given small amounts over a period of time, probably to make it look like her cancer had come back."

"Wow!" Brodie said, not knowing what to make of this. "So she was being poisoned slowly."

"Yeah," Jason said. "Whoever did it knew how much to

give her so it wouldn't be too lethal until they were ready to finish her off."

"They?" Brodie said.

"Remember the bruises on her wrist? She was definitely held down, and whoever held her down could not inject the needle at the same time."

"I have two murderers and a bunch of people who couldn't give me a straight story," Brodie said, sounding disgusted. "Jason, do me a favor and keep this under wraps about there being two people involved."

"No problem, Brodie. Until I hear from you, my lips are sealed," Jason said.

Brodie walked around Betty's bedroom, not sure what he was looking for, when he spotted a small spoon, one you would use for feeding a baby. He picked it up with his handkerchief and looked it over. There was some residue on it. He could almost guarantee it was rat poisoning because it was a beige color and the spoon had been hidden. Why would anyone hide a baby spoon? He placed it in a plastic bag and searched the room further. He flipped Betty's mattress off the bed and found a manila envelope. He opened it and found pictures of Candy and Paul. The first picture was of Paul hugging Candy, his hand was on her buttocks. The second picture was Candy sitting on Paul's lap, her head resting on his shoulder and her hand inside his shirt on his chest. There were a few more pictures of Paul and Candy, nothing provocative, just enough to put suspicion in your mind that it was more than a father and daughter relationship. Brodie put the pictures in his shirt pocket. He looked around the room at all the angels, and that's when a thought came to him.

Betty was being poisoned slowly by someone who came by all the time. Samantha was here on a regular base to bring her mother small gifts. Could someone who bought her mother small gifts all the time kill her own mother? There was only one way to find out he had to talk to Samantha.

Brodie knocked on Samantha's door three times and was getting ready to leave when Penny opened the door.

"Detective, I'm sorry it took me awhile to answer. I just got out of the shower when I heard the knock and tried to hurry and dress," Penny said all out of breath.

"Can I come in?" Brodie asked

"Yes, of course. I'm so sorry. Come in," Penny said as she opened the door and stepped aside, still trying to dry her hair with the towel.

"Is your mother home?" Brodie asked, looking around the small house. It was very crowded but clean. The living room was the first room you walked into when you entered the house. There was a love seat and sofa, a TV stand with a TV on it, and that was all of the furniture because you could not fit anything else in the tiny room.

"I'm sorry, Detective, my mother isn't home. She works until five," Penny answered, watching Brodie scan the room.

"I have a few questions for you. Can we sit and talk?" Brodie asked. Not waiting for an answer, he sat on the sofa with his big legs stretched out in front of him.

Penny sat on the love seat. "What about?" she asked nervously.

You said you saw your mother in the garden as soon as your grandmother went up to take a nap. "Is that true?"

Brodie asked, looking into Penny's eyes hoping to get a hint of something.

"Yes, Detective, that's true. But as I said, I never had the chance to talk to my mother because Candy called me and I went looking for her," Penny said without looking directly at Brodie.

"I forgot to ask you, did you ever talk to Candy?" Brodie asked, watching Penny's demeanor.

Penny looked right into Brodie's eyes as hers welled up in tears. "I'm sorry, Detective. I'm trying to forget that yesterday ever happened. But to answer your question, no I didn't talk to Candy. I couldn't find her. She called me that once and not again so I couldn't follow her voice. I tried calling her, but she never answered."

"When did you hear the nurse screaming?" Brodie asked, not knowing what to believe.

"Um, it had to be about ten to fifteen minutes later," Penny answered as she wiped the tears from her eyes.

"Something is not adding up here, Penny, and I need the truth because I'm getting very angry; and believe me you won't like me angry," Brodie said sternly.

Penny's eyes got big, and a frown came across her face. "Detective, I am being totally honest with you," Penny said in a nervous voice.

"The story Candy told me is the opposite of yours. She told me as soon as she called you the nurse screamed and you came from the back of the house and your mother from the side. Neither one of you was in the garden," Brodie said, trying to sound angry, hoping he would get some answers.

"What?" Penny said. "I never saw Candy. I couldn't find

her, and the nurse didn't scream for at least ten minutes or so of Candy calling me. I don't know why she lied," Penny said with a shocked expression on her face.

"You did not see your mother in the garden, did you, Penny?" Brodie asked more delicately.

Penny put her head down and sobbed. "No, Detective, I didn't. I'm sorry, but I swear that's the only thing I lied about," Penny said as she wept.

"Why did you lie? If your mother did nothing wrong, there is no reason for you to lie," Brodie said softly.

"I don't know. Everything was happening so quickly. My grandmother was dead. You said we were all suspects. I didn't want my mother to be blamed."

"Did you see your mother at all?" Brodie asked.

"Yeah, she was making my grandmother a cup of tea. I didn't say anything because I didn't want anybody pointing a finger at her."

"Why would anyone point a finger at your mother?" Brodie asked.

"Because she was in my grandmother's room giving her tea and making sure she was all right."

"I see," Brodie said. "Could you have your mother call me when she comes in from work?" Brodie said as he got up to leave.

"Sure, Detective," Penny said. "My mother loved Gram. She was there all the time. She would never harm her," Penny said with tears in her eyes.

"Let me ask you one more question," Brodie said. "What do you think about your uncle Paul and Candy's relationship?" Brodie watched as a shocked looked came over Penny's face and she put her head down.

"It's okay," Penny said quietly. "I mean they're close like any father and daughter," Penny said with her voice cracking.

"Penny, is there anything you would like to tell me? If something is wrong with Candy and your uncle Paul, I'm here to help any way I can," Brodie said, concerned.

"I'm sorry, Detective, but I don't know what you mean," Penny answered without looking up at Brodie.

"Good enough," Brodie said. "But if you think of something or there is something you would like to talk to me about, let me know."

"I will, Detective," Penny said and then closed the door after Brodie left. Penny stood against the door sobbing for a few minutes. She didn't know what to do. She may have gotten her mom in trouble for lying, and she had to confront Candy for lying about her. Penny sat on the couch just as Walter came in.

"What's wrong ?" Walter asked when he saw Penny sitting on the couch with tears coming down her face.

Penny told him everything that she and Brodie had talked about.

"Wow," Walter said. "First of all I know Mom would never harm Gram; we just have to make Detective Brodie know. As long as Candy stays out of that situation; you know Uncle Paul."

"How are we going to make the detective believe Mom is not a murderer?" Penny sobbed. "I blew it."

"No, you didn't," Walter said as he rubbed Penny's back.

"The detective is a smart man. He knows you were only trying to protect Mom, and I'll figure something out. Don't worry."

"Who do you think killed Gram?" Penny asked between sniffles.

"Somebody without feelings," Walter said, sounding a bit angry.

"Does he know about Gram having you arrested?" Penny asked, concerned.

"Uncle Paul and Candy made sure he did," Walter said with a snicker.

"Oh my god!" Penny said. "What did he say?"

"Nothing really. I was honest with him and told him everything," Walter said. "Listen, I don't want to talk about this anymore. Let's get some lunch."

. . . . .

Brodie walked into the forensic lab and handed Jason the spoon he had found.

"What's this?" Jason asked.

"You tell me," Brodie said. "Call me when you do." Brodie waved his hand and walked out the door.

Brodie was waiting for Samantha to call when the phone rang. "Brodie here," he said as he picked up the phone.

"Detective Brodie, this is Carman's mother, and I need to know what's going on with my daughter's case."

Brodie put his head down. Carman was the twelve-year-old girl that went missing. "Ms. Ramosa, I am terribly sorry, but I am working on a murder case. And I sent my investigators out looking for your ex-boyfriend, Mr. Morales," Brodie said.

"Detective Brodie!" Ms. Ramosa yelled into the phone. "My daughter has been missing for two weeks. You were working on my daughter's case first. I want you to find my daughter."

"Ms. Ramosa, I understand how you feel, but a murder case has precedence over a missing child," Brodie said, trying to sound calm and sympathetic.

"Why? Is that dead person going somewhere? I don't think so. My baby girl could be halfway across country by now," she sobbed.

Brodie didn't have the heart to tell her that her daughter could be in another country by now.

"Ms. Ramosa, I'm truly sorry. I'm still working on your daughter's case, just not full-time. I'm not going to forget your daughter. I promise," Detective Brodie replied.

Ms. Ramosa started sobbing, "Thank you, Detective, please keep me updated, and I have your promise that you won't forget my daughter."

Brodie hung up the phone, feeling terrible that he didn't have any new information for Ms. Ramosa. The phone rang just as he went to the bulletin board and took another look at Carman Ramosa. It was a school picture. She had a big smile on her face showing off her braces. She had big brown eyes and long lashes, and her dark brown hair was pulled back into two ponytails. Brodie turned from the picture and went to pick up the phone. "Brodie here."

"Detective Brodie, this is Samantha Carlton. My daughter said you wanted to talk to me."

"Hello, Mrs. Carlton, would you like to come into the

station or would you like me to come out to your house?" Brodie asked, as he flicked his pencil on his desk.

"What is this about, Detective? And I don't want you to question my children without me being present," Samantha snapped.

Detective Brodie knew Penny would tell her mother everything. "I'm investigating a murder. It means I can talk to whom I want when I want," Detective Brodie snapped back.

"I don't have time to talk to you, Detective. I need to plan my mother's funeral," Samantha said coldly.

"Make the time!" Brodie yelled.

"Listen, Detective, I am very busy. I'll see what I can do," Samantha said a little calmer.

"Do you have rats?" Brodie asked out of nowhere.

"What?" Samantha asked, shocked. "Why would you ask me a question like that?"

"I'm sorry," Brodie said. "When I was at your house, I noticed your garbage was ripped. It had holes in it as if a small rodent did it," Brodie said trying to call her bluff. "I have some rat traps if you're interested?" Brodie asked, hoping to get the answer he was looking for.

"Oh," Samantha said. "I'm sorry, Detective; I have had a long day. Thank you anyway. I have rat poison I have been putting out," Samantha said tiredly.

Brodie had a big smile on his face. *Hook, line, and sinker*, he thought to himself. "The poison doesn't seem to be working," Brodie added, trying not to let her know he was on to her. "You sure you don't want the traps?" Brodie asked.

"No, thank you, Detective. I'm going to try increasing the

poison. If there is nothing else, Detective, I am really busy, and I promise to call you soon."

"Please do," Brodie said, eager to hang up. "Don't wait too long. I do need you to clear up a few things for me." After Samantha promised she would, Brodie hung up. He then made a call to the prosecutor's office.

Brodie banged on Samantha's door with two uniform officers and a search warrant.

Samantha looked shocked when she opened the door. "What is going on?" she asked in a shaky voice.

"Mrs. Carlton, we have a search warrant," Brodie said as he brushed past Samantha with the detectives in tow.

"What!" Samantha yelled. "A search warrant! Why?"

"Please sit down, Mrs. Carlton, and I'll explain after the search," Brodie said. He walked into the kitchen, and under the sink he found the rat poison. He put it in a plastic bag and went up to the bedrooms.

Walter's room was a mess. His clothes were on the floor, his desk and bed piled with stuff. He looked through the drawers and closet. He then made his way to the pile of junk on the desk and bed and found nothing. He then went to Penny's room. He saw a picture of her in a cheerleader outfit and pom poms hanging from the wall. He had no idea that Penny was a cheerleader. He then looked closer at the picture and noticed the date was from last year. He found nothing in Penny's room. He walked into Samantha's room and looked around. Everything was very well organized. He stood near her bureau, looking at the collection of angels. He spotted her hairbrush and took a few strands of hair and placed them in a plastic bag. He then went through her nightstand. As he was going through her nightstand something caught his eye. It was a window seat, and he saw a corner of a piece of paper hanging out from under the cushion. He walked over to pick up the cushion, and the whole seat lifted up, showing a storage compartment. Inside he found a bottle of morphine and some syringes. He bagged them and continued to search. He found a bunch of letters from her ex-husband begging to come home.

He walked into the kitchen just as the two officers came up from the basement. "Find anything?" Brodie asked.

One of the officers handed Brodie a plastic bag. Inside was a piece of paper. Brodie took it out using a handkerchief. On the top it said *different ways to get rid of someone.* Brodie read the list:

1. suffocation
2. electrocution
3. drugs
4. poison

Brodie could not believe what he was reading. He walked into the living room to find Walter and Penny sitting next to Samantha on the couch. Brodie walked over to Samantha.

"Samantha Carlton, you're under arrest for the murder of Betty Thompson."

"What?" Samantha yelled. "You can't be serious. Why would I murder my mother?"

Brodie started reading Samantha her rights as one of the officers handcuffed her.

"Why are you doing this?" Walter yelled. "My mother

could never hurt anyone. She is not a murderer. You need to look at my uncle," Walter yelled even louder.

"Walter!" Samantha yelled. "Don't make accusations. Please call your uncle and have him meet me at the police station." Penny clung to her mother sobbing. "It's going to be all right. Your uncle will straighten this mess out," Samantha said as she kissed Penny on the cheek.

The two officers walked Samantha out to the car. Brodie watched as they put her in the backseat. He turned around and looked at Penny and Walter. "Is there anything you need?" Brodie asked.

"Yeah," Walter said coldly. "My mother out of cuffs."

"I'm sorry, Walter, but I cannot do that," Brodie said sadly.

"Then investigate my uncle, please," Walter begged.

"I will," Brodie said. "I'm still investigating everyone."

"Then why arrest my mother?" Penny sobbed.

"Because of the evidence I found, I believe she had some part in your grandmother's death. But I also believe she wasn't alone. That's why I'm still investigating."

Brodie drove away with Penny and Walter looking on. He hoped he was wrong and that there was a reasonable explanation for everything.

"I'm not saying a word until my lawyer gets here," Samantha snapped as Detective Brodie walked into the interrogation room.

"That's your right," Brodie said as he sat at the table across from Samantha.

"Then leave," Samantha snapped.

"I'm going to wait right here until your lawyer gets here," Brodie said as he sat at the table looking into Samantha's eyes. "By the way do you know it was rat poison that killed your mother?" Brodie looked in her eyes for something that would tell him he was wrong. He was usually a good judge by reading people's eyes. That's what made him a good detective. All he saw was anger in Samantha's eyes no fear, just shock and anger.

"What? No, Detective, I didn't," Samantha said with all the color draining from her face.

"I hope you're not questioning my client without me being present," Paul stated as he walked over and gave his sister a kiss on the head.

"I have not said a word to your client," Brodie said, looking up at Paul who took a seat near his sister. Brodie watched their actions. Samantha seemed intimidated by Paul. She kept her head down as he whispered in her ear. Brodie noticed Paul put his hand on hers, and she pulled away quickly as though his hand were made of fire.

"Detective, I want to know what kind of evidence you have against my client." Paul asked, opening his brief case and taking out a notepad.

"That's what I would like to discuss with your client," Brodie said, sharply letting Paul know he might intimidate his sister but he sure wouldn't intimidate him.

Paul looked hard at Brodie. "Okay, Detective." He then turned to Samantha. "Only answer the questions I tell you to answer," he said in a demanding voice. Samantha just shook her head okay.

"Why did you have a bottle of morphine and a syringe hidden in your window seat?" Brodie asked, looking into Samantha's eyes.

Samantha looked at Paul who shook his head yes. "It wasn't hidden. I keep it there because of Walter's friends. I don't trust them, and the reason I have it is because I used to take my mother to my house a lot and she never remembered her morphine, so I always kept some at my house for her," Samantha answered coldly.

"How did you get the morphine and syringes? You can't just go into a pharmacy and buy them," Brodie said.

Samantha looked at Paul again, and he shook his head yes. "I got it from her doctor. I explained to him that my mother was always forgetting it, and he gave me some to leave at my house," Samantha answered.

"What's with this?" He tossed the paper he found at Samantha.

"I never seen this," Samantha yelled. "My children have a lot of friends that come in and out."

Brodie sat writing in his notepad before he asked the next question. "What about the rat poison? I talked to your neighbors, and none of them ever seen a rat or had any problems with them."

Samantha looked at Paul. He shook his head no.

"Give me a minute with my client," Paul said.

Brodie left the room while Paul and Samantha talked in private. Brodie could see through the glass on the door that Paul and Samantha were in a heated discussion. Brodie watched as Paul slammed his fist on the table and Samantha cried. "Something is not right," Brodie said to Officer Hayden, who was standing next to Brodie.

"Maybe she wants to confess, and he doesn't want her to," Hayden replied.

"No, it's more than that. I can't put my finger on it, but something is going on," Brodie said, running his hand through his hair.

"You can come back in, Detective," Paul said as he opened the door.

Brodie looked at Samantha. Her eyes were puffy, and she was definitely scared.

"Mrs. Carlton, is there anything you would like to tell me before I book you for murder?" Brodie asked.

"Yes," Samantha said, looking up at Paul with trembling lips.

Brodie looked at Paul who glared at Samantha with daggers in his eyes. "What is it that you want to tell me?" Brodie asked.

Samantha looked at Paul with wide eyes and then put her head down. "I didn't kill my mother. I love her," Samantha sobbed.

"Is that all you wanted to tell me?" Brodie asked, looking up at Paul who seemed more relaxed.

"Yes, Detective, that's it," Samantha cried.

Brodie had been so sure this woman was guilty, but now he had serious doubts. "Officer Hayden will take you to booking. A female officer will meet you there. If there is anything at all you want to talk to me about, please have one of the officers downstairs get in touch with me," Brodie said, pleading.

"Thank you, Detective, but if my client has anything to say she will talk to me first," Paul said, directing his statement toward Samantha.

Brodie sat at his desk, trying to figure out if he was wrong about Samantha. If he was then why did she have rat poisoning when there were no problems with rats in her neighborhood. And why was Paul risking his sister's life behind bars when he obviously knew something. Brodie called it a day and headed home. There was nothing more he could do there except give himself a headache.

THREE

Brodie played with his sons until their bedtime and then sat on the couch with Betty's journal, hoping to find some answers.

"Long day?" Jessica asked, rubbing Brodie's shoulders.

"Every day's a long day," Brodie said as he took Jessica's hand in his and kissed it.

Jessica kissed Brodie on the neck. "I'll leave you alone to read the journal," Jessica said as she squeezed Brodie's shoulder. "Promise me after this case we will do something as a family," Jessica said.

"I promise," Brodie said. "And thanks for putting up with me." He then pulled Jessica into his arms and kissed her lips.

Jessica kissed him back and then pulled away. "Read your journal, and after this case you're all mine," Jessica said, planting one big kiss on Brodie's lips before going upstairs to the bedroom, leaving Brodie alone.

Brodie opened the journal and started reading where he had left off. After reading for half an hour, Brodie was ready to call it quits when the next paragraph grabbed his attention.

> I tried to talk to Paul about his relationship with Candy.
> He yelled and called me sick. I tried to explain to him
> how it looked to others and that I wasn't accusing him
> of anything, but he stormed out of the house and told
> me if I said anything to anybody about my sick, I would
> be sorry.

Brodie thought for a minute. *If she mentioned it to anyone,*
who would that be?

Samantha maybe she told Samantha, and that's what
Paul was angry and worried about.

Maybe he thought Samantha would say something to me
to help her case. "What about the rat poison," he muttered.
"It always comes back to that." Brodie read more, hoping to
find some answers when he came across another interesting
paragraph.

> The only person I trust to confide in is Harvey, but I'm
> not sure if I should tell him that Paul tried to have me
> committed so he can take all my money. Thank God
> Dr. Kendal kept everything quiet. He refused to sign
> the papers Paul gave to him to have me committed and
> told Paul if he tried to take it to court he would fight
> it on my behalf. Harvey would be furious at Paul if I
> told him. I believe William knows. He seems to know
> everything that goes on before I do. I don't know what
> Paul is going to try next.

Brodie closed the journal. William knows everything, hmm.
I think it's time I paid him a visit tomorrow. Brodie stood up
and stretched and then went up to bed. Jessica was fast asleep.
He crawled into bed and cuddled next to her and drifted into

a deep sleep, dreaming of twelve-year-old Carman. She was reaching for him, begging for him to help her. Brodie woke up in a cold sweat. The sun was streaming through the window. He could hear his boys getting ready for school.

"Mommy, I can't find my other shoe," Tommy yelled.

"Try cleaning your room," Brodie said as he swatted his T-shirt at him. "And then maybe you will find it." Brodie tucked his T-shirt into his jeans as he walked into the kitchen.

Jessica put his coffee on the table. "Tough night?" she asked. "You tossed and turned all night."

"I'm sorry," Brodie said as he picked up his coffee cup and took a long sip. "No breakfast. I need to get an early start," he said as he hooked his badge to his jeans and took his gun out of his lock box and put it in his holster.

"You have to eat something," Jessica said as she handed him two pieces of toast.

"Thanks. I'll eat this in the car. Boys, I'll see you tonight. Be good." he then gave Jessica a kiss and hug. "I'll see you tonight."

Jessica watched as he climbed into his car and drove off. She closed the door and leaned against it. "Come on, boys, time for school," she yelled. "It's getting late."

Brodie pulled up the long driveway of Betty Thompson's estate. He parked in front of the house and got out.

"What can I do for you, Detective?" William, the gardener, said.

"I came to talk to you," Brodie said. "I hope you can answer a few questions for me."

"Sure, Detective. What do you want to know?" William

asked as he laid the plant parts he was carrying by the side of the house.

"I understand you know just about everything that goes on around here," Brodie said.

"That I do. I always keep my ears to the grindstone, if you know what I mean," William said with a chuckle.

"Yes, I do," Brodie said. "And I want you to tell me everything you know, starting with Paul."

"Detective, if you want me to tell you everything, this could take awhile," William said with a big grin.

"I'm not going anywhere," Brodie said. "I have all the time you need."

"Okay then, let's go to my cottage on the back side of the property where we can have some privacy."

Brodie followed William to the back of the property. They walked up the path of a small white cottage.

"Would you care to sit outside or inside?" William asked.

"It's a nice day; we'll sit outside on your porch," Brodie said as he took a seat on one of the chairs.

"Okay," William said as he sat in the seat opposite Brodie. "Where do you want me to start?"

Brodie took out his notepad. "I want to know what you think of Paul's relationship with his daughter Candy."

William smiled. "Everyone believes Paul is having a sinful thing going on with his daughter," William chuckled.

"You don't believe he is?" Brodie asked.

"Well that depends on what you're asking me," William said. "If you're asking me if Paul is having a sexual relationship with his daughter, my answer is no, but if you're asking me if he is having a sexual relationship with Candy, my answer is yes," William said with a sly grin.

"What," Brodie said, alarmed. "Candy is not Paul's daughter?"

"No, she's not. Mrs. Thompson had an affair with Paul's former boss and got pregnant," William answered.

"Who knows about this?" Brodie asked.

"Nobody. They all assume Paul is the daddy," William said with a snicker.

"Interesting," Brodie said as he wrote in his notepad. "Why did Mrs. Thompson have the baby, knowing it wasn't her husband's?"

"She didn't want it, but Paul forgave her for having an affair so she agreed to have the baby because Paul wanted it. Go figure, huh," William said, shaking his head.

"Does Candy know this? That Paul is not her father," Brodie asked, looking confused.

"Yes, she knows. That's why she is sleeping with Paul," William said. "She believes that he is in love with her and she is in love with him. Poor girl, if she only knew the truth."

"And what is the truth?" Brodie asked.

"You are not going to believe this," William said with a low whistle. "Paul is also sleeping with Penny his niece," William said. "He's a dog, a real pit bull."

Brodie was taken aback. He couldn't believe what he was hearing.

"Do you want to know more?" William asked.

"Yeah," Brodie said. "I need to know everything." Brodie ran his hand through his hair and sat back.

"Walter knows about his uncle and sister. That's why he

is so angry. The night he got drunk, he walked into the shed to get the lawnmower to mow the lawn for Betty, because I can't push that thing anymore, and caught his uncle pulling at his sister's panties. Penny was crying. Walter yelled at his uncle. And Penny came running out, crying."

"Did you see all this?" Brodie asked.

"Sure did, right from my window had a bird's-eye view," William said, pointing to his window.

"Why didn't you report this, or at least say something to somebody?" Brodie asked in an angry voice.

"Paul spotted me in the window. He told me if I breathed a word to anyone my job here would be finished and he would make it look like I was a child predator who was trying to watch Penny change into a bathing suit."

Brodie moaned, "So what happened when Walter yelled at his uncle?" Brodie asked.

"As I said, Penny jumped up crying and ran. Paul grabbed Walter and told him if he so much as breathed a word to anyone he would make sure it was his last and then he would torture his mother and sister. Walter was so angry he was shaking. He pulled away and ran down toward the stream. Paul adjusted his tie and walked away as if nothing had happened."

"Wow," Brodie said. "Samantha Carlton is in jail for the murder of Betty. Do you think she is capable of murder?" Brodie asked.

William looked stunned. "Samantha, no way! She adored her mother. She always tried to protect her from Paul's temper."

"What do you mean?" Brodie asked.

"Whenever Paul couldn't get money from Betty, he would turn ugly and start yelling and calling her names. Samantha always managed to get him out of the room and away from her."

"Did Samantha ever talk about having trouble with mice or rats in or around her house?" Brodie asked.

"No, but Paul had given me some rat poison and asked me to give it to Samantha, so I assumed she had some kind of rodent problem," William said.

"He asked you to give rat poison to Samantha? Why did he ask you?" Brodie asked, confused.

"He was getting in his car when he spotted me. He called me over and asked me to give it to her, saying that she would be there anytime but he couldn't wait since he had an appointment."

Everything was starting to make sense, Brodie thought. "What did Samantha say when you gave her the bag of rat poison?" Brodie asked.

William laughed. "She looked at me like I had just grown two heads and asked me what she wanted rat poison for. I told her Paul had asked me to give it to her. She just shook her head and put it in her car and mumbled something about talking to Paul."

"Can you tell me what you observed the day Betty was murdered, if anything?" Brodie asked.

William rubbed his chin, thinking for a minute. "Just before Betty went upstairs, Paul went up and then came down with Betty's teacup. I remember because I thought finally he was going to do something nice for his mother and make her a cup of tea."

"Did he make her tea?" Brodie asked.

"No, that was the strangest thing. He put a tea bag into the cup and then left it on the table and went outside," William said.

"Did you see anyone make her a cup of tea?" Brodie asked.

"When Betty went up to nap, Samantha came in, and I told her that Betty would feel better after a nice cup of tea and that Paul had left her cup with a tea bag in it on the table," William explained.

"Did she bring Betty up the tea?" Brodie asked.

"Yes, she did, after mumbling what an idiot Paul was," William said, laughing.

"Do you know if the box of tea bags that Paul used is still here?" Brodie asked.

"I don't know," William said. "You will have to check with Natalie, the housekeeper."

"Thank you, William. You don't know how much you helped me today," Brodie said as he stood and shook William's hand.

"It was my pleasure, Detective," William said as he followed Brodie down the stairs. He watched Brodie head for the house as he turned and went back to work in his garden.

Brodie found Natalie cleaning out the cupboards in the kitchen. He cleared his throat so he wouldn't startle her.

"Detective, what can I do for you?" Natalie asked.

"Paul Thompson had some tea bags here the day Betty was found dead. Would you happen to have them?" Brodie asked.

"Paul took the tea bags out of the cupboard right after

Betty was found dead," Natalie said. "I thought it was kind of strange, but who am I to question?" she said.

"He took the whole box?" Brodie asked, disappointed.

"Yes, all but these three that must have fallen out of the box," Natalie said as she handed them to Brodie.

Brodie smiled. "Thank you," he said as he placed the tea bags in a plastic evidence bag.

.　.　.　.　.

"Run tests on these for me," Brodie said as he tossed the bag to Jason.

"What am I looking for?" Jason asked as he picked up the bag of tea bags.

"Rat poison. It seems that Paul Thompson has been using these tea bags to make his mother tea, and when she died Paul took the tea bags with him all but these three that the housekeeper found," Brodie explained.

"Well," Jason said, "another twist in the case."

"Let me know what you find immediately," Brodie said.

"You got it, buddy, but didn't you just arrest Samantha Carlton?" Jason asked.

"Yes I did, and I'm on my way to talk with her. Don't forget two people committed this crime," Brodie said.

Samantha Carlton was sitting on the cold metal bench in the holding room where Brodie had asked permission to speak with her. "How are you doing?" Brodie asked.

"How do you think I'm doing, Detective? I'm behind bars, not knowing what's happening to my children," Samantha snapped.

"Who is taking care of your children?" Brodie asked.

"My brother, Paul," Samantha said sadly. "Detective, what do you want?"

"You want to go home to your children? I can help you," Brodie said.

"How?" Samantha said, curiously.

"By telling me the truth, for starters. Why did Paul give you the rat poison?" Brodie asked, looking into Samantha's eyes. He watched the color drain from her face and her lips tremble.

"Where did you hear that from?" Samantha asked, trying not to let her voice crack.

"That's not important," Brodie said. "If you want to get out of here, you need to start talking."

"I don't know what you're talking about," Samantha snapped, trying to sound convincing.

"Why are you protecting your brother?" Brodie asked.

"I'm not protecting anyone," Samantha said softly. "I really don't know what you're talking about."

"Penny is staying with your brother?" Brodie asked, concerned.

"Yes, Detective, I already told you that," Samantha answered, annoyed.

"Mrs. Carlton, what I'm about to tell you is hard, but believe me I'm not doing this to hurt you. I'm only concerned about Penny's welfare," Brodie said.

"Penny! What's wrong with Penny?" Samantha asked, alarmed.

"You need to have a long talk with Walter," Brodie said as he moved closer to Samantha and talked softly. "He walked in on Paul trying to molest Penny."

Samantha turned white. Tears filled her eyes and ran down her cheek. "You liar!" she yelled. "Paul would never molest his niece," Samantha cried.

"It's not me you're calling a liar. It's your son. Do you think he would make something like this up?" Brodie made it sound like Walter told him what Paul did instead of the gardener, but he had to break her.

Samantha cried big gulping cries. "Why?" she yelled and punched the table. "Why would he do something like this?"

"I don't know, Mrs. Carlton, but you need to talk to me so I can get you out of here and get you back home with your children," Brodie said.

"Okay," Samantha said. "But you need to protect me and my children," Samantha said, worried. "Promise me you will protect us."

"I promise. I won't let anything happen to you or your children," Brodie said softly. "I need to have the prosecutor in here. She's the only one who can dismiss any charges against you. She's in the hall. I'll have the guard get her," Brodie said. Brodie had already talked with Cindy Patterson, the prosecutor, on the evidence he had that he hoped would help Samantha and nail Paul. Cindy had warned that the only way she would consider dropping the charges against Samantha was if Samantha told everything she knew without playing games.

Cindy walked into the holding room. She sat across from Samantha, looking at her. She knew Samantha had been crying. Her eyes were red and puffy. She looked frail and tired. Cindy hoped Samantha would talk because it was Paul she wanted behind bars. She had been investigating

Paul for a long time ever since allegations surfaced about him molesting his daughter Candy as well as complaints of sexual harassment on other teenage girls in the neighborhood. None of the teenage girls wanted to press charges and go to court for fear of retaliation. They were willing to go until Paul was questioned, and then they would change their minds. Cindy knew Paul had gotten to them somehow.

"Mrs. Carlton, I need you to tell us everything," Brodie said.

"Before you begin I need to turn on my tape recorder," Cindy said.

Samantha nodded her head yes and then looked at Brodie.

"I have your promise that nothing will happen to my children?" Samantha asked in a shaky voice.

"We will give you protection," Cindy said. "Mrs. Carlton, are you familiar with the allegations against your brother from three teenage girls in his neighborhood?" Cindy asked.

Samantha looked startled. "No," she said. "What allegations?"

"It appears your brother has a thing for teenage girls," Cindy said with a sneer. "The three teenage girls said Paul had been sexually harassing them and grabbing certain parts of their bodies. Unfortunately, Paul got to them, and they all dropped the accusations," Cindy said with disgust. "We need to get him off the streets. Please help us as well as yourself," Cindy said, more sympathetic.

Samantha looked down. "Okay, I will tell you everything I know."

Cindy smiled and looked over at Brodie, who sat quietly.

She then turned on her recorder. "Okay, Mrs. Carlton, please state your full name."

"Samantha Rose Carlton," Samantha said softly.

"Thank you, Mrs. Carlton. But when I ask you questions, I need for you to speak a little louder," Cindy said, smiling. "Start from the beginning and tell us about the rat poison."

Samantha looked over at Brodie, who gave her a reassuring nod. She rubbed her hands together, looked down, and cleared her throat. "After William gave me the rat poison, Paul called and told me to hang on to it and if anybody asked to tell them I was having problems with rats. I was a little confused and asked Paul what it was for, and he told me to mind my business and not say a word to anyone."

"Why didn't you push the issue?" Cindy asked.

"You don't know Paul. He can become very violent," Samantha stated.

"I don't understand," Cindy said. "When Detective Brodie found the rat poison and arrested you, why didn't you say anything then?"

"At the time I didn't know it was rat poison that killed my mother," Samantha said as her eyes welled up with tears.

"When Detective Brodie told you rat poison killed your mother, why didn't you tell him the truth then?" Cindy asked.

"Because Paul came into the room, and I needed a chance to talk with him alone."

"Detective Brodie left us alone for a few minutes, and I asked Paul about the rat poison. He got angry and told me not to say a word, saying that he would explain everything at a later time and that he would take care of everything and if I did breathe a word to anyone he would put my children in foster care and make sure I rot in prison," Samantha said, sobbing.

"I need to know about his relationship with his daughter Candy," Cindy said.

"Candy is not his daughter," Samantha said. "Trisha broke down and told me that she had an affair and became pregnant. She wanted an abortion, but Paul was adamant about her having the baby."

"Paul signed the birth certificate. That makes him Candy's father," Cindy said, a little annoyed. "Did Trisha suspect that he was fooling around with Candy?"

Samantha looked down at the table. "Please don't do anything to Trisha. She is torn between protecting all her children."

"What do you mean?" Cindy asked, looking a bit confused.

Samantha started to sob. "She went to New York to visit her mother and returned home early to surprise Paul." Samantha stopped and wiped her eyes with a tissue and then continued. "She was the one who got surprised when she walked in on Paul and Candy naked in bed. She started screaming. Paul jumped up and punched her in the mouth, splitting her lip open."

Cindy looked horrified. "What did she do then?"

"Paul told her he would put her in the hospital if she said anything to anyone. Trisha started yelling that he could do whatever he pleased to her but he would never touch her daughter again. She reached for the phone to call the police, and Candy yanked it out of her hand, yelling that she was in love with Paul and she would do whatever it took to protect him," Samantha said sadly.

"What did she mean by that?" Cindy asked, concerned.

"Trisha tried to explain to Candy how wrong and sick this was and that what she mistook for love was really lust, something her father put into her head. Candy started yelling that it wasn't sick because Paul was not her father and that she was in love with him. Trisha got angry and told Candy she was going to put her in the hospital for help and put Paul behind bars. Candy got angry and told Trisha if she did anything to Paul she would burn the house down while she slept."

"Wow," Cindy said. "But that still doesn't explain why she didn't put Paul in jail or Candy in the hospital as she said."

Samantha took a long breath. "Paul told her if she even tried to put him in jail she would pay big time because she had no proof of anything except her word and he would put her in a mental hospital and put Stanley and Cora in foster homes. Trisha flipped out. She started throwing things at him, telling him that Stanley and Cora were his children and asking how could he do such in evil thing."

"What was his response to that?" Cindy asked.

"He didn't care. He had a reputation to protect, and he would protect it no matter what. As far as he was concerned, Stanley and Cora were liabilities that could be eliminated if need be. Trisha went into a state of shock. She couldn't believe that Paul could be capable of such cruelty toward his own children."

"When did Trisha talk to you about all this?" Cindy asked.

"About four months ago. She was devastated, and I was in shock to think my brother could be capable of something so sick."

"What about murder? Do you think he could be capable of murder?" Cindy asked.

"I don't know. I really don't want to believe he is, but I really don't know," Samantha sobbed.

"Your sister-in-law does. That's why she hasn't said anything to anyone. She fears for her children's lives," Cindy said.

"What if I told you your mother knew?" Brodie said, who had sat quietly through the interview.

"What, how do you know she knew?" Samantha asked, shocked.

"I have her journal and some photos that were hidden under her mattress. The photos are not explicit but do look suspicious."

"Oh my god!" Samantha groaned. "If he could threaten to kill his own children, then he could kill his own mother if he thought she knew."

"I need you to do something for me, and if you pull it off I'll have you out of here tonight," Cindy said, looking into Samantha's eyes.

"What is it?" Samantha asked, worried.

"I need you to call Paul and tell him you need to talk to him, and I want you to get him to tell you that he gave you the rat poison. I will wire you up to a tape recorder. I need this on tape."

"Promise me I will be able to leave here tonight and you will put me and my children in a safe place," Samantha said.

"I promise you will go home tonight and we will protect you and your children if you get him to confess that he gave you the rat poison and if you can get him to talk about Candy."

FOUR

Samantha sat in the holding room waiting nervously for Paul, hoping he couldn't see her wires. Her children's lives depended on her pulling this off because if he suspected anything she had no idea what he would do to her children.

Paul walked into the room carrying his briefcase. "What do you want to talk to me about?" Paul asked as he sat across from Samantha.

"You are my lawyer," Samantha said, trying to sound brave. "I need to know what you're doing to get me out of here. I can't take being in here, Paul," Samantha cried.

"I'm doing everything I can. Please calm down," Paul said, concerned.

"Where did the rat poison come from?" Samantha asked, trying not to sound nervous.

"Don't worry about where it came from," Paul snapped.

"What do you mean don't worry? I'm stuck in here not knowing how my kids are or if I even have a job when I get out," Samantha sobbed.

"I'm sorry, Samantha. I had a long day. Maybe I shouldn't have given you the rat poison, but I didn't know where else to put it," Paul explained.

"Why did you have it?" Samantha asked, trying not to show her joy at him admitting to giving it to her.

"I found it in Trisha's car and got worried that she wanted to kill me," Paul said, rubbing his eyes.

"Has this got something to do with Candy?" Samantha asked, knowing she was entering deep water.

Paul turned red. "What are you talking about?" he yelled.

Samantha was very scared but couldn't back down. Not know she had opened a can of worms, she planned on continuing. "Mother told me. She also showed me pictures of you and Candy that she had taken," Samantha said, calling his bluff.

Paul turned three shade of red. "Pictures!" he barked. "That rotten woman! Who else knows about this?" he yelled.

"Nobody," Samantha said. "I have not said a word to anyone. Paul, please tell me what's going on. I promise not to say a word to anyone," Samantha pleaded.

"Where are the pictures?" Paul demanded.

"Tell me what's going on, and then I'll tell you where the pictures are," Samantha said, trying to sound brave even though her insides were like jelly.

"I trust you, and you trust me. Is that it?" Paul sneered.

"You could say that," Samantha said.

"Okay, you win," Paul said. "But if you ever say a word to anyone, your children will become orphans," Paul snapped.

"I won't say a word to anyone, Paul. I promise," Samantha said in a shaky voice.

"I am not Candy's father," Paul stated.

Samantha tried to sound surprised, "You're not! Oh my god!" she cried.

"Trisha had an affair with my old boss. I found out and was going to divorce her but couldn't because I was too much in love with her. Then we found out she was pregnant. I always wanted more kids so I convinced Trisha to have the baby. Believe me when I tell you I didn't plan on having an affair with Candy it just happened," Paul said, looking down at the table.

"When did it start?" Samantha asked curiously.

"Candy found out she was not my daughter. She overheard Trisha and I arguing one night, and Trisha blurted out that she should have told Kevin my old boss, the guy she had an affair with, that Candy was his daughter."

"Oh no, poor Candy," Samantha moaned, meaning it.

"Candy was devastated. She cried on my shoulder for over an hour, and then she looked me in the eye and told me she was glad I wasn't her father because she could stop feeling guilty about the feelings she had for me. I asked her to explain, and she told me that she was in love with me. She stood up and took off her clothes."

"Why didn't you stop her, Paul? She was obviously very confused," Samantha said, shocked.

"I couldn't. I was in total shock. And then she started to undress me, and one thing led to another. And before you ask, yes, I did feel guilty for the time I cried, but I could not stay away from her. Just being with her felt right," Paul said with a grin on his face.

"My god, Paul," Samantha stammered. "You raised her

like she was your daughter. How could you have sex with a young girl?" Samantha asked, confused.

"First of all, she's not my daughter, and second she wanted me. I was sick of looking at Trisha's body getting old and out of shape. Candy's is firm and beautiful," Paul said, smiling.

Samantha couldn't listen to anymore. "It's over," she said. "It's all over."

Paul looked confused. "What are you talking about?" he asked.

"As she said, it's all over," Brodie said as he entered the room with Cindy and two uniformed officers.

"Paul turned white. He glared at Samantha, "You no good piece of trash!" he yelled. "I'll get you for this," he screamed as the officers handcuffed him and Brodie read him his rights.

Samantha stood there with tears streaming down her face. Her body started to shake as she sat down in the nearest chair.

"A few people want to see you," Brodie said as he looked down at Samantha, smiling.

Samantha looked confused. "Who?" she asked.

The door opened wider, and Penny and Walter walked in smiling.

Samantha jumped up and grabbed both her children and wrapped her arms around them, crying.

"Is there any room for me?"

Samantha looked toward the sound of the voice, and there stood Trisha with a big smile on her face and tears running down her cheeks. "Always room for you," Samantha said as she reached for Trisha.

Brodie cleared his throat. "Sorry to interrupt, but this is far from over. Paul didn't work alone."

Samantha looked pale. "What are you saying? That there is another killer out there?"

"That's exactly what I'm saying," Brodie said.

Trisha kept her head down and never said a word. Tears slowly ran down her cheeks as she wiped them away.

"Mrs. Thompson, I'm sorry, but I have a feeling you know who the second person is just as I do."

"Please, Detective," Trisha cried. "She is just a child. Paul has had a lot of influence over her. If she did help him, she still may be innocent," Even as Trisha said those words, she knew Candy had helped Paul kill her mother.

"Mrs. Thompson, the chances of Candy not being involved are slim," Cindy said. "If we can get her to talk with us, we hope we can work out a deal."

"What kind of deal?" Trisha asked between sobs.

"Instead of prison time we could get her psychiatric treatment in a good hospital," Cindy said.

"Candy will never turn on Paul. She believes she is in love with him," Trisha cried.

Samantha put her arms around Trisha. "We will talk to her, and maybe she will realize what Paul really is," Samantha said, knowing it was a long shot.

"If she refuses to talk, we will turn things around," Cindy said.

"What do you mean?" Trisha asked, confused.

"Please sit down, Mrs. Thompson, and let me explain," Cindy said calmly. "We can tell Candy that Paul confessed and made a deal, that he blamed everything on her to get a lighter sentence and is willing to testify against her."

"Do you think that will work?" Trisha asked hopefully.

"It has never failed," Cindy said, smiling. "I have a townhouse for the two of you and your children to stay in. It's on the outskirt of town."

"Do you really think it's necessary for us to leave our home?" Trisha asked.

"Yes, I do," Cindy said. "Paul will be granted bail because he has a law firm and has been an upstanding citizen. He is not considered a flight risk."

"What? Not a flight risk! He committed murder and had a sexual relationship with a fifteen-year-old girl!" Samantha snapped. "He also tried to molest his own niece."

"I understand your anger, but he has not been convicted yet. They're only allegations," Cindy said, trying to sound calm. "I don't think I'm going to charge him with trying to molest Penny. I don't want to turn the attention away from the big picture, how he seduced and used Candy to help him commit murder."

Trisha and Samantha just looked at each other and sobbed.

Cindy felt for them. She planned on fighting that Paul be held without bail, but she knew from all her past cases that he would be granted bail.

They all forgot about Penny and Walter standing in the corner until Penny spoke up. "Thank you for not dragging me into it."

"I didn't say I would not charge Paul. I want to wait and see how things progress," Cindy explained. "If I think the jury is not buying Candy's story about being seduced, then we may have to use you."

"I understand," Penny said, looking at the floor. "When do we go to the townhouse?" she asked in a scared voice.

"I need to pick up Candy first. I don't want her to know about the townhouse just in case she makes contact with Paul," Brodie said, who had sat quietly at the end of the table.

"Penny, Walter, I need your promise that you will tell no one where you will be staying or about any conversation that took place in this room," Cindy said sharply.

"I promise," Penny said softly as she walked over to her mother and put her hand on her shoulder.

"Me too," Walter said, from the corner of the room. He stood with his back against the wall and his hands shoved in his pockets.

"Good," Cindy said. "Trisha, I need you to bring Cora and Stanley to the townhouse. I will give you directions. Don't say anything to them about what's going on."

"How do I do that? I can't very well have all their clothes in suitcases and tell them we're going for a drive," Trisha asked, confused.

"Tell them their dad is waiting for them in a cabin by the lake, that he wanted a spontaneous family vacation. Something tells me they're used to your husband doing things like this," Cindy said with a hint of humor in her voice.

"What about Candy?" Trisha asked.

"Detective Brodie will take care of that," Cindy said. "I think we should get going. Paul is entitled to one phone call, and I don't want it to be to Candy."

"How do we know he has not called her already?" Trisha asked, worried.

"I left word at the station not to let him have a phone call for at least two hours," Cindy said, as they all walked out of the room and to the locked gate. Cindy showed her badge and Samantha's release papers, and they were all sent through. Once outside Cindy gave Trisha and Samantha directions to the townhouse. "I will meet you there in one hour," Cindy said as she climbed into her car.

All the way to Trisha's house, Brodie had no idea what he was going to say to Candy or how she would take the news of Paul's arrest. Just before he got to Trisha's house, an idea came to him. He called for a female officer for back up. He watched Trisha drive into the local coffee shop where she was told to wait.

Brodie knocked on the door, and Candy opened it. He had hoped she would.

"Detective, what can I do for you? My parents are not home," she said quickly.

Brodie was happy but didn't show it. He knew Paul has not called her yet. He cleared his throat. "Candy Thompson, you're under arrest for the murder of Betty Thompson," Brodie said.

Candy turned white. Tears ran down her face. "What are you talking about?" I want my father. He will straighten this out," Candy cried.

"Your father has also been arrested," Brodie said.

The female officer handcuffed Candy and led her out to the car.

"What's going on?" Stanley asked as he and Cora came to the door after hearing Candy crying.

"We're taking your sister in for questioning, no big deal," Brodie said, hoping that they bought it.

He knew Cora would because she lived in her own world, but Stanley was a different story.

"Can you take her to the station without my parents' permission?" Stanley asked.

"I have your father's permission. He is at the station waiting for Candy. I just have to clear up a few discrepancies between her and Penny's stories," Brodie said, trying to sound convincing. "Shouldn't you to be packing?" Brodie asked to throw them off.

Stanley and Cora looked confused. "Pack for what?" Stanley asked.

"Your dad said something about you all going away on vacation for a few days. He asked my permission because of the ongoing investigation. Nobody is supposed to leave town. He asked to take you all away for a while," Brodie said, hoping Stanley believed him.

"Cool," Cora said, bouncing up and down. "Did he say where?" she asked.

"No, I'm sorry. He didn't. Please do me a favor and don't tell your dad I told you. He probably wants to surprise you," Brodie said.

"No problem, Detective," Stanley said with a smile on his face.

As Brodie drove by Trisha, he beeped the horn. She waved and started her car up to go home.

. . . . .

Brodie walked into the interrogation room. Candy was sitting at the table with her hands folded in front of her. Her eyes were puffy and swollen from crying. She looked terrified Brodie thought. "Hello, Candy." She looked at Brodie with the saddest eyes he had ever seen.

"Where is my dad?" she asked crying. "I want to see him."

"Candy, you're in a heap of trouble," a voice said from the door. Cindy walked in, holding a notepad, and sat across from Candy.

"Who are you?" Candy asked in a shaky voice.

"I'm Cindy Patterson, the prosecutor and your only hope of staying out of jail," Cindy said in a stern voice.

"What do you mean?" Candy asked. "I didn't do anything wrong," she cried.

"That's not what your father says," Cindy said, trying to bluff Candy into a confession.

"My father? What are you talking about? My father would never accuse me of anything," Candy said, confused.

Cindy pretended to read her notes. "According to your father, you wanted your grandmother out of the way. She knew about your relationship with your father, or should I say stepfather," Cindy said, cocky.

All color drained from Candy's face. "I don't know what you're talking about," she stuttered.

"Candy, don't play games with me," Cindy snapped. "I don't like games, and I don't have time for them. If you want to stay out of jail, you had better start talking. Your stepfather made a deal for less jail time."

Candy sat quietly. Tears rolled down her cheeks. "What kind of deal?" she asked softly.

"He will testify against you, saying it was all your idea and you're the one who fed your grandmother rat poison, slowly poisoning her, and that you came on to him sexually. He tried to push you away, and you wouldn't take no for an answer."

"My father would never do that to me," Candy snapped.

"Then tell me, Candy, how do I know about your sexual relationship with your father?" Cindy asked more softly.

Candy didn't respond. She sat with her head down, shaking.

"Candy, he is going to hang you out to dry, while he serves a little time and then is out back on the street. Help us, Candy, please," Cindy asked.

Candy sat crying. "I don't believe you. My father would never do that to me."

"No, Candy, your father won't, but what about Paul, your lover?" Cindy asked softly. "Candy, you're going to jail for murder. You will not see the light of day for the rest of your life. Paul will be out in ten to fifteen years because of his testimony against you."

Candy sobbed harder. "If I tell you everything, how much time will I get in jail?" she asked.

"If you tell us everything and agree to testify against Paul, you won't go to jail. But you will have to go to psychiatric hospital for a while," Cindy said.

"For how long?" Candy asked, sobbing softly.

"I don't know," Cindy said. "But it will be a whole lot less then you would serve if you went to prison."

Candy cried. "Okay, I'll do it. I'll tell you everything." Candy cried harder.

Cindy put her arm around Candy's shoulder. "I know how hard this is. Take your time, and we will get through this. You are doing the right thing."

"I didn't want to kill my grandmother. I loved her. I really did." Candy stopped and cried.

Cindy waited for Candy to compose herself before she asked the next question. "Why did Paul want her dead?" Cindy asked in a soft comforting voice.

"Because she knew about us," Candy stated. "Paul said if she told anyone it would ruin him and then we couldn't be together anymore. But we were only supposed to give her rat poison to kill her memory. That's what he said."

"You just called him Paul," Cindy said.

"He hated it if I referred to him as dad. I don't blame him. It just wasn't right. He's not my dad."

"What would you refer to him by if not your father?" Cindy asked.

"My boyfriend," Candy said, wiping her tears away.

"Tell me how everything came about with the planning of giving the rat poison to your grandmother," Cindy said.

"Paul came to my room one night. His face was red, and he was very angry. I asked him what was wrong, and he started to shake. He told me that grandmother knew about us. I didn't see a problem, and I told him that maybe it was for the best because we could finally be together." Candy stopped, looked down at the table, and rubbed her hands together.

"I bet that comment didn't make Paul happy," Brodie said as he sat at the table with the tape recorder running.

"No, it didn't," Candy said. "He was angry and told me if anyone found out it would destroy him and that we could never be together. I cried, and he told me he had a plan. If I helped him we could be together forever. We would move away and start a new life because he would have all the money he needed."

"His mother's money," Cindy said.

"I told him no when he told me the plan with the rat poison," Candy cried.

"He refused to talk to me for days. Then he came to me crying that his career was over because Gram was going to tell all. He said that I had to help him."

"You mean to kill her?" Cindy asked.

"Yes, but at the time I didn't know that," Candy said, more composed. "I promised him that night I would help him. He told me when he was ready he would let me know and to ask no questions until then."

"When did you discuss poisoning your grandmother?" Cindy asked.

"Three days later. He came home with a bag of rat poison and told me to hide it in my room. I asked him why there was so much. With a big smile on his face, he said that it was for our future. I was confused and told him he was making no sense. That's when he told me not to worry. I had a feeling it was bad."

"Why didn't you stop him right then and there? Why did you go along with his plan?" Brodie asked.

"At first I thought he was joking. And when I found out he wasn't, I tried to talk him out of it. He told me if I didn't help him then we were through and we would never have a life together."

"What was your part in it?" Brodie asked.

"Paul gave Aunt Samantha a box of tea bags that we had put rat poison in and told Aunt Samantha that grandmother was out of tea bags so he had picked some up for her."

"He knew Samantha was going to see your grandmother on a regular basis," Cindy said.

"Yes," Candy said. "He went to see Gram the same morning he gave Aunt Samantha the tea bags and took all of Gram's tea bags and banana nut muffins and trashed them. He knew Aunt Samantha always made Gram a cup of tea and gave her a banana nut muffin."

"What did he do to the muffin?" Cindy asked, curious with this new revelation.

"He sprinkled a little rat poison on top and wrapped them back up," Candy said with tears welling up in her eyes again.

"What happened the day your grandmother died?" Brodie asked.

Paul told me that he and Gram had gotten into a big argument the night before over Walter and he couldn't take it anymore and that we had to finish Gram off that day. I asked him what he was talking about. He told me that he would find me later and we would talk.

"Did you see Paul later?" Brodie asked.

"Yes. He was very upset. He said he had gone to check on Gram and she was in a lot of pain and wanted him to end her life. He begged me to help. He gave me a little spoon with rat poison on it. He told me to take it up to Gram's room and hide until Aunt Samantha brought up her tea and when she left to go over and pretend to stir Gram's tea and drop the poison in her cup."

"How did he know Samantha would bring your grandmother tea?" Cindy asked.

"Whenever Gram didn't feel good or had a bad headache, Aunt Samantha always brought her tea. It helped calm her down."

"What happened after Samantha left the bedroom?" Brodie asked.

"I was hiding in the hall cupboard. I went into Gram's room. She looked over and smiled at me." Candy stopped and sniffed a few times and wiped the tears from her eyes. "I walked over to Gram and asked her how she was doing. She told me she was in a lot of pain and she wished it would all just go away. I dropped the poison in her tea when she closed her eyes and hid the spoon under the bed. I just wanted all her pain to end," Candy cried.

"We're almost done, Candy. Please finish," Cindy said.

"Paul came up a few minutes later. I was sitting next to Gram crying because I managed to get her to drink all her tea and she didn't look so good."

"You poisoned her what did you expect," Brodie snapped.

Cindy gave Brodie a look. She didn't want him to blow it now. They were all most done, and she needed Candy to say that Paul was in the room and helped with the final stage of the murder. "Take a deep breath, Candy, and then finish."

Candy took a deep breath. "Paul called me into the hallway. He was angry that I was crying and told me to stop because if anyone saw me crying before Gram was found disorientated, it wouldn't look good. I went into the bathroom to wash my face. When I came out, Paul was filling a syringe with morphine. He told me to hold both her arms really tightly in case she tried to fight."

"Did she fight?" Cindy asked.

"No, not really. She moaned a little when Paul stuck her with the needle and pulled her arm a bit, but she never fought." Candy started to cry. "I just wanted her pain to go away."

Cindy gave Candy a few more minutes before she asked, "What did the two of you do after you gave her the morphine?"

I watched Gram for a few minutes as her face relaxed, and I didn't see any more pain. Paul grabbed my arm after a minute or two and told me to go downstairs and look for Penny and hang out with her."

"You didn't have a chance to hang out with Penny, did you?" Brodie asked.

"No. I called Penny, and within a few minutes the nurse screamed. We were not expecting her to find Gram that quickly," Candy said sadly.

"Candy, I need to place you in protective custody. You will be going to the state hospital for treatment," Cindy said.

Candy shook her head yes and looked up with tears in her eyes. "My mom is going to hate me," Candy cried.

"Your mother knows what's going on. She is deeply worried and concerned for you; she loves you very much.

"Can I see my mom?" Candy asked between tears.

"Not for a few days or so. You need to get settled first," Cindy said.

Candy just shook her head yes. "Okay, just tell my mom I love her."

FIVE

Cindy and Trisha both reached the townhouse at the same time. Samantha was already there. She opened the door when she saw them pull up.

"What's going on?" Stanley asked as he looked at Cindy and Samantha. "Where is my dad?"

"Come inside, and I will explain everything," Cindy said.

Cora, who was usually bubbly, looked confused as she slowly walked up the stairs and into the house.

Once they were all in the house, Cindy asked them to sit down. She then directed her attention to Stanley and Cora and began to explain about their father and sister. Cora sat in total silence as tears ran down her cheeks, and Stanley put his head in his hands.

Trisha put her arms around both kids, but Stanley shook her away.

"You had an affair on dad, and now all our lives are ruined," Stanley yelled, turning red in the face.

"Stanley, my affair had nothing to do with all of this," Trisha said in a tired voice.

"The heck it didn't!" Stanley yelled. "If you hadn't had an affair, Dad wouldn't be screwing Candy and they wouldn't have killed Gram." Tears streamed down Stanley's face. He punched the wall and then fell against it.

"Stanley, I want you to look at something," Cindy said as she handed Stanley some papers.

"What's this?" he asked as he snatched the papers from Cindy.

"Statements from teenage girls accusing your father of sexual harassment, Cindy said. "Stanley, if it wasn't Candy, it would have been some other young girl."

Stanley stood in the corner and cried. Trisha went to him, and Stanley grabbed and hugged her tight. "I'm sorry, Mom. I'm so sorry," Stanley cried.

"It's okay, baby. It's okay," Trisha cried, holding her son and stroking his back.

"What's going to happen to my sister?" Cora asked, who sat there with tears staining her face.

"We will get her the help she needs," Cindy said. "You must remember she is as much a victim as the rest of you."

"How could my dad do this to her?" Cora cried.

"I don't know, honey. I just don't know," Trisha said as she and Stanley went to Cora and hugged her.

"I'm going to go and leave you all some privacy," Cindy said. "Cora and Stanley, nobody must know where you are, understood?" Cindy asked.

They both shook their heads yes.

Brodie got home just in time to help Jessica get the boys ready for bed. After they were tucked in, Brodie went into the kitchen and opened a can of beer.

"Want something to eat?" Jessica asked. "I have leftover meatloaf and potatoes. I'll warm them up if you want."

"That sounds good," Brodie said. "I made the arrest on Betty Thompson's murder," Brodie said tiredly.

Jessica stopped putting the potatoes in the dish and turned to Brodie. "Wow, that's great. Who is it?" she asked as she turned to finish Brodie's dinner.

"Paul Thompson," Brodie said.

"What? Her son? Oh my god. Why would he kill his own mother? That's horrible!" Jessica said in a shocked voice.

"What's horrible is what he did to his daughter, excuse me, stepdaughter," Brodie said, correcting himself.

"What did he do to her?" Jessica asked curiously.

"He had a sexual relationship with her. He convinced her that he was in love with her and the only way they could be together was to do away with Betty," Brodie said with disgust.

"Oh my god!" Jessica said as she placed his dinner in front of him. "That poor child! What's going to happen to her?"

"She will go into the state hospital for help after her testimony against Paul," Brodie said and then shoved a fork-full of potatoes in his mouth.

"Will she testify against him?" Jessica asked, a little worried.

"Yes, we have her confession on tape as well as Paul's part in it," Brodie said.

After dinner Brodie snuggled on the couch with Jessica and fell asleep. He had the same nightmare as the night before, the twelve-year-old missing girl Carman. She was reaching for him, and he was trying to get to her but was being held back by some unknown source. She kept crying, "Help me, please!" He tried but couldn't reach her. He woke up in a cold sweat. Jessica was sleeping on his arm. The sun was just starting to stream through the window. Brodie gently pulled his arm out from Jessica.

Brodie started a pot of coffee and then jumped into the shower.

"Daddy, I need to use the bathroom," Tommy said as he banged on the bathroom door.

"Hey, sport, not so loud. Let your mom sleep," Brodie instructed.

"Who's going to give us breakfast?" Brandon asked as he came out of his bedroom.

"I think the two of you are old enough to pour cereal into a bowl with milk," Brodie said sternly. "Without making a mess," he said a little louder.

"Oh, Dad, we hate cereal. Mom buy's that junky kind," Tommy said.

"It's not junky. It's good for you. Mom doesn't want your teeth rotting out. That's why she buys the cereal with no sugar," Brodie explained.

Brodie made his coffee as the boys poured their cereal. Brodie cut up some bananas for their cereal to give it a little flavor.

"Dad, can we watch cartoons?" Tommy asked.

"Keep it down low," Brodie said.

"Why didn't you wake me up?" Jessica said as she lifted her head off the couch.

"Because everything is fine," Brodie said. "The boys ate. They're getting dressed. And then they will finish watching cartoons, so you can relax with your coffee," Brodie said as he gave Jessica a kiss. "I need to go," he said. "I'll be home early."

"Thank you for taking care of the boys," Jessica said as she stood up and put her arms around Brodie's neck and kissed him.

Brodie was at his desk when a fax came in. It was from his friend, a private investigator he had asked to follow up on Carman Ramosa for him. Brodie read the fax and laid it down just as the phone rang. "Brodie here."

"Detective Brodie, this is Ms. Ramosa. I need to know what's going on. I have not heard from you."

"Ms. Ramosa, I was going to call you. I just received information that Carman was seen in Texas two days ago. It is good news because we know that she is still alive," Brodie said.

"Detective, I always knew my baby girl was alive. I want to know what you're going to do to bring her home."

"I'm sending a fax to the Texas state police with a picture of Carman, and they will pick it up from there," Brodie explained.

"Detective, I want you to go there and bring back my baby," Ms. Ramosa demanded.

"Ms. Ramosa, I can't. It's out of my jurisdiction," Brodie explained. "And I'm still on this murder investigation."

"I want my baby back, Detective!" Ms. Ramosa cried.

"I will get her home to you. I will personally call the state police myself," Brodie said. "I'll bring her home, Ms. Ramosa."

"Thank you, Detective. I needed your reassurance," Ms. Ramosa said and then hung up.

Brodie called the state police in Texas and informed them about Carman Ramosa and that she was last seen in their state. After the police promised that they would look for her," Brodie hung up. He then faxed her picture over to them.

Brodie had to get to the courthouse. Paul Thompson's

lawyer had managed to get him into court for a bail hearing. *It must be nice to have connections,* he thought.

Paul sat at the defendant's table dressed in a navy three-piece suit, looking very smug.

Cindy sat at the prosecutor's table in a pinstriped skirt, ready to do battle.

Brodie sat in the front row, watching as both sides argued about Paul's bail. Cindy informed the judge that his family was in fear of him getting out.

And Paul's lawyer said, "That's untrue. Paul never harmed his family in any way." In the end Paul got a one-hundred-thousand-dollar bail. Brodie was upset as well as Cindy.

"With a bail bondsman and his mother's will being read in one hour, he could be back on the street by tonight."

Brodie and Cindy were both asked by Trisha and Samantha to go to Betty's lawyer's office with them. They were fearful that Paul would get out and meet them there.

Brodie pulled up the same time Cindy did. She had Trisha and her two kids in her car, and Brodie had taken Samantha and her two kids in his car.

Trisha and Samantha both looked around worriedly. "Don't worry," Brodie said. "He won't be out this early."

"You don't know Paul," Trisha said. "He has good friends that will give him money, knowing he is going to get it back from his mother's will."

"Let's go inside," Cindy said. "If he does get out, I don't want you standing here on the sidewalk."

The lawyer shook everyone's hand and then sat behind his desk and opened a folder "Let's see," he said. "I think we will start with the children. "To all my grandchildren who have brought me so much joy, I leave one hundred thousand dollars apiece to be used on college if you choose to go. If not you will receive the money on your twenty-fifth birthday. Candy my love, if you are still with your father (you know what I mean), you will receive nothing."

"Trisha, my beautiful daughter-in-law, I leave you one million dollars on the signing of your divorce from Paul. If you remain married to Paul, you will receive nothing. You are too smart and beautiful to have to put up with him."

"My darling daughter, I leave you my home and cars, as well as one million dollars to get on with your life."

"Harvey, my best friend, I leave you two hundred thousand dollars and all my love."

"The rest of my devoted staff, I leave you all fifty thousand dollars each."

"I also leave the police department fifty thousand dollars and various charities, which my lawyer will take care of."

"My son, Paul I leave you my bill of all the money you borrowed from me. It comes up to seventy thousand dollars. My lawyer will collect it from you and donate it to the children's center for sexually abused children."

"Can I please have a copy, so I can take it to the prison and give Paul a copy?" Brodie asked.

"Do you want a copy of the whole will?" the lawyer asked.

"No, just Paul's part. I don't want him knowing what his family received," Brodie said.

On the way to the prison, Brodie was smiling. He was hoping without this money Paul wouldn't be able to make bail. Brodie entered the visiting area and saw Paul sitting at the table waiting for him.

"Hello, Paul," Brodie said as he sat down.

"What do you want?" Paul snapped.

"I came to give you the reading of your mother's will," Brodie said as he watched Paul's demeanor change from somber to a smile.

"Well, let's see," he said as he snatched the paper from Brodie's hand. As he read the paper, a cloud came over his eyes, and his face turned red. "Is this some kind of joke?" he yelled. The guards started to come over, but Brodie put his hand up.

"No joke," Brodie said. "That's your mother's last will, and you will repay the money," Brodie said as he leaned back in the chair with a smug expression on his face.

"And how am I supposed to pay this kind of money back? If you haven't noticed, I'm not in a place of employment," Paul snapped.

"No, but you do have a Porsche that will be auctioned off. If that doesn't bring enough money while you're in here, you will work, and the money will go to pay off your debt," Brodie said.

"Auction off my Porsche? You can't do that!" Paul snapped. "And even if you could, what do you mean 'if it doesn't bring in enough money'? Do you know how much that's worth?" Paul snapped.

"Yes, I can auction off your car to pay a debt. This is a legal lawsuit against you. And yes, I know how much your car is worth, but when you auction it off, you take the best price," Brodie snapped back.

Paul sat back in his chair. "I can't believe she did this to me," he snapped. "What did my family get?"

"I can't tell you that. All I can tell you is they will be living comfortably for life as long as Trisha divorces you," Brodie said.

"What are you talking about? My wife won't divorce me!" Paul snapped.

"She has already started divorce proceedings with your mother's attorney," Brodie said with a smug look on his face.

"You're really enjoying this, sitting there so smug. This is not over yet. Candy will get me off; wait and see," Paul said with an evil grin on his face.

"I'm sorry, Paul, but didn't your attorney tell you that Candy turned state's evidence against you," Brodie said.

"Candy would never do that to me, never!" Paul yelled.

"I think you need to talk to your attorney," Brodie said as he got up to leave.

"What did you do to her?" Paul snapped.

"We gave her a deal she couldn't refuse," Brodie said with a smile and then walked away, hearing Paul yell after him.

"This isn't over, Detective. This is far from over. I will be out. I don't need my mother's money," Paul yelled.

Brodie smiled as he was walking out the door and almost walked into Cindy.

"That went well," Cindy said with a smile on her face.

"Yes, it did. What are you doing here?" Brodie asked.

"Meeting with Paul and his attorney to see if we can plea bargain to end this case," Cindy said.

"Plea bargain! Why?" Brodie asked, shocked. "We have all the evidence to hang him. Why do you want to plea bargain with that creep?"

"Detective, I understand how you feel, but if there is a tiny loophole that he can slip through, I want to stop it,"

Cindy explained. "Besides I don't think he will go for it, and if he doesn't, there will be no other deals."

"What kind of deal are you offering him?" Brodie asked.

"He pleads guilty to murder, and we drop the statutory rape charge. He will serve at least twenty years. If not, with the statuary rape he will serve thirty to thirty-five years," Cindy said.

"So either way he is going away for a long time," Brodie said. "Are you afraid of Candy backing down?" Brodie asked.

"She believes she is in love with him. Anything is possible. I don't want to take any chances," Cindy said.

"Good luck," Brodie said as he walked away and then stopped. "Paul never said anything about this meeting."

"Because he doesn't know yet," Cindy said. "I just got done talking to his attorney."

Just then Paul's attorney showed up. It was one of his buddies from his law firm. Mr. Nolan.

"Nice to see you again," he said as he extended his hand out.

"Mr. Nolan, good to see you too," Cindy said as she reached to shake his hand.

"Detective Brodie, nice to see you. I didn't know you would be here," Mr. Nolan said as he reached to shake Brodie's hand.

"I know you?" Brodie asked.

"I have seen you around the police station and courthouse. You have a good reputation, Detective."

"Detective Brodie was just leaving," Cindy said. "Shall we go inside?"

"Good day, Detective. It was a pleasure to meet you," Mr. Nolan said.

"Yes, you too," Brodie said, wondering if Mr. Nolan would feel the same way when he found out that Brodie was the one who busted his client and wouldn't give up until he was locked away for good.

Cindy walked into the visiting room with Mr. Nolan by her side. She saw the shocked expression on Paul's face.

"What's going on?" he asked as they both sat down across from him. He watched Cindy open her notepad and his lawyer open a folder. "Is anyone going to answer me?" Paul asked again.

"Mr. Thompson, I'm here to offer you a plea bargain," Cindy said.

"A plea bargain," Paul snapped. "I'm not guilty. Why would I want a plea bargain?" Paul yelled louder.

"Paul, please just hear her out," his lawyer instructed. "It's a good deal. I wouldn't be here if it wasn't."

"Okay, fine, what is it that you could possibly say to make me plead guilty to a crime I didn't commit?" Paul snapped.

"Candy Thompson turned state's evidence against you," Cindy said.

"Prove it," Paul snapped. "Prove to me that Candy turned on me because I don't believe it. I didn't believe it when the detective told me, and I don't believe it now," Paul said as he sat back in the chair with his arms folded against his chest.

Cindy pulled out a tape recorder and played it. Paul sat shocked as he listened to Candy's confession implicating him.

"What did you offer her to make her lie about me?" Paul snapped. "That little witch is lying to save her own neck."

"Why would she confess to murder if she was trying to save her own neck?" Cindy asked.

"How would I know? She's a selfish little witch, that's why," Paul yelled.

"Here's the deal," Cindy said. "You plead guilty to murder, and I will drop the statutory rape charge against you."

"What? Are you crazy? Why would I plead guilty to murder? I'm innocent," Paul snapped.

"If you do you will receive twenty years in prison. If you don't you will receive thirty to thirty-five years, and with Candy's testimony I can guarantee you will be convicted," Cindy said.

"Paul, I think this is a good deal. I think you should take it," Mr. Nolan said.

"This is my life we're talking about, not yours," he yelled at his attorney. "I want to go to trial," Paul snapped.

"Okay," Mr. Nolan said. "Trial it is." He closed his folder and looked at Cindy. "No deal, we're going to trial," he stated.

"I think you're making a mistake, but it's your life," Cindy said. "I'll see you in the courtroom." Cindy headed for the door and was about to leave when she heard Mr. Nolan talking to Paul.

"I'll have you out of here in thirty minutes. All the guys pitched in for your bail. I need to go pay the bondsman, and you will be out."

"Great," Paul said. "This place is making me sick. I can't sleep or eat. I can't wait to get home."

"Paul, your family is not there," Mr. Nolan said.

"Where are they?" Paul snapped.

Cindy walked back into the room. "I have them in protective custody," Cindy said. "You are not allowed to look for them or contact them in any way. If you do I will have you back in here so fast that you won't have time to breathe."

Paul stood there, shocked. "Okay, fine," he said. "I don't need them." He walked back over to the table and sat down, rubbing his head.

Cindy walked out, listening to Paul complain about getting a raw deal. She knew she had to protect Candy. Once he found out she was in the hospital, he would be there. Once outside she called Brodie on her cell phone.

"He's out on bail!" Brodie yelled.

"I need Candy protected," Cindy said. "Once he finds out where she is, he will try to contact her."

"I'll send a uniformed officer there, and I will also talk to them to make sure nobody gets in to see her. And if Thompson shows up, I want to be notified immediately," Brodie said.

"Thanks, Brodie," Cindy said. After she hung up she knew she had to go let Trisha and Samantha know that Paul was out on bail.

Brodie could not believe that Paul could get out on bail. Who in their right mind would bail him out? Brodie called the hospital where Candy was and left orders that Candy was not allowed visitors while her case was still under investigation, and if Paul Thompson were to show up there to call Brodie right away.

Brodie knew Paul could find Candy through his attorney.

The phone rang and made Brodie jump because he was deep in thought. "Brodie here."

"Brodie, this is Jason. I have something for you."

"What is it?" Brodie asked.

"The tea bags did contain rat poison, but that's not all. There were also traces of aftershave."

"What?" Brodie asked "How did aftershave get into the tea bags and why?" Brodie asked, shocked.

"It is not on the tea leaves themselves. It's on the outside of the bag," Jason explained. "Whoever put the poison in the tea bags handled it after putting on aftershave."

"Can you tell me what kind of aftershave it is?" Brodie asked.

"We're working on that now," Jason said. "It smells like Old Spice. One of my lab techs noticed the smell when he picked it up. I told him to run some tests, and it came back as aftershave."

"This is great news," Brodie said, smiling. "Fax me what you have and let me know as soon as you find out what kind," Brodie said.

As soon as Brodie hung up, he called Cindy on her cell phone and informed her of Jason's findings.

"Let me know as soon as you find out what kind it is," Cindy said. "This is good news," she said into the phone. "There is no reason for him to handle a tea bag by the bag itself unless he was doing something to it. Most people only touch the string," Cindy said with a big smile.

"I was thinking the same thing," Brodie said.

"Keep me in touch," Cindy said and then hung up.

S I X

Trisha and Samantha were sitting at the table drinking coffee when the four children came into the room.

"Can we talk to you?" Penny said in a quiet voice.

"Of course you can," Samantha said. "Sit down and tell us what's on your mind."

Penny sat next to her mother, and Cora sat next to hers. Both boys stood next to the wall with their hands in their pockets.

Cora spoke up first, "When Candy gets out of the hospital, we all want to give her half of our money that Gram left us."

Trisha and Samantha looked at each other. "Gram left Candy money too. Why would you want to give half of yours away?"

Stanley stepped forward. "We don't blame Candy for what Dad did. She was influenced by him."

"When she does come home, she is still going to need a lot of counseling, and we want to make sure she has enough money for it," Stanley said.

"Besides everything she is going through, she deserves this money to help her build a good future," Walter said.

"I just need enough to open a garage when I graduate high school and then get my mechanics license."

"I only need enough to open my own beauty shop after I get my beauticians license," Penny said.

"I'll have an athletic scholarship for college, and I figure after college fifty thousand will pay for med school," Stanley said.

Trisha had tears in her eyes. "I want you all to keep your money. I have more than enough to help Candy out."

"We know that, Mom," Cora said. "But this is something we want to do. Let's face it, I haven't been the best sister in the world. Maybe if I were a better sister she wouldn't have turned to Dad for support. I was always worried about me, and this whole situation really opened my eyes. I owe Candy this much and more. Please, Mom, I don't need the money. I'm going into business with Penny."

Trisha was crying. She had had no idea Cora had felt this way and carried this kind of guilt for the last few days. No wonder she has been so quiet lately."

"Cora, you are not to blame here. None of us are. It's your father that should be ashamed for what he has done, not any of you," Trisha said, wiping the tears from her eyes.

"When did you all plan out your futures?" Samantha asked. "The last I knew, none of you had a clue on what use wanted to do with your life."

"Ever since all this started, it made us all think about what we could have and what we could lose," Penny said.

Nobody said a word. They all looked at each other wondering what the others were thinking.

The doorbell made them jump. "Don't answer it," Samantha said quietly. "Let me peek out and see who it is."

Samantha peeked out the window, while everyone else stood close by holding their breath.

Samantha turned and smiled. "It's okay; it's Cindy," she said as she opened the door. Everyone took a deep breath.

"Hello, everyone," Cindy said as she entered the room. "I have some news that you are not going to like."

"Let's go into the kitchen and have some coffee," Trisha said. "I always take bad news better with coffee." After Trisha made everyone some coffee, they all looked at Cindy.

"Paul is out on bail," Cindy said

Trisha turned white. "I shouldn't be surprised he always comes out ahead," Trisha said with tears welling up in her eyes.

"He is not coming out ahead this time. I promise," Cindy said. "He won't get away with this."

"What about Candy? What if he finds her?" Trisha cried.

"Detective Brodie and I took care of that. Candy has a uniformed officer around the clock outside her room, and she isn't allowed any visitors. Candy is safe. Don't worry," Cindy said in a calm voice.

"Why can't she come here with us?" Cora asked. "We will protect her."

"I know you will. But she is safer in the hospital, and we're trying to get her as much counseling as possible before trial," Cindy explained.

"Are you going to see her?" Cora asked with tears starting to come down her cheeks.

"Yes, I will be seeing her from time to time," Cindy said.

"Tell her we all love and miss her," Stanley said. "And tell her we don't blame her for anything. We just want her to get better," Stanley said with his voice cracking a bit.

"I will. I promise. I arranged for a tutor to come here three days a week to help you keep up with your schoolwork so you don't fall behind," Cindy said.

"I thought we were on an extended vacation," Walter joked, trying to lighten the mood.

"Not on my watch," Cindy laughed. "I need to get going. Just keep your eyes and ears pealed. I don't think he will find you, but I don't want to take any chances," Cindy said.

"We will," Stanley said. "I won't let him anywhere near my family," he growled.

"Stanley, please don't play hero. If you see him, call 911 immediately," Cindy ordered. "He's a dangerous man, and I don't want you hurt."

"I'm sorry. I'm not going to play hero unless he makes it through the door," Stanley said.

"Good enough. "Stay away from the windows. And one more thing, I told the tutor to ring the bell once and then knock twice, and from now on that's what I will be doing. Don't open the door unless you hear that code." Cindy opened the door, looked around, and then left.

· · · · ·

Paul took in a deep breath of fresh air as he walked to Mr. Nolan's car. "Tell me something, Bob," Paul asked. "Where are they holding Candy?"

Mr. Nolan looked at Paul. "I'm not going to tell you because you will find yourself back in jail. Paul, please stay at home. Don't do anything that will hurt your trial."

"Bob, I'm concerned about my daughter. That's all. They filled her head with so much nonsense she's probably not sure what is going on, poor girl. I just want to send her flowers, just to let her know I love her and that Daddy will never turn on her because of these lies everyone put into her head."

"That's fine, Paul. Give me the flowers, and I'll take them to Candy," Bob said.

"Really, you'll do that? And will you tell her I'm not mad at her, that she is still Daddy's girl?"

"Yes, I will. Here's a flower shop. Go pick out what you want," Bob said.

Paul went in and picked out a dozen yellow roses, Candy's favorite, and then wrote on the card, *Daddy's girl always and forever* and underlined *girl*.

When Bob pulled up in front of Paul's house, Paul invited him in for a drink.

"No thanks, Paul, another time. I promised my wife I would be home early," Bob replied.

"Are you going to take those flowers to Candy first? I don't want them to wilt before she sees them."

"Yes, I'm going there right now," Bob said he waved to Paul and drove off.

Paul ran to the garage and jumped in his old Buick. He never knew why he had saved this car. He had bought it when he was a law student. Bob would not recognize him in this heap of junk. He pulled out and drove up the street. Knowing the intersection as he did, he knew Bob would be stuck there for a while. Sure enough there was Bob's car. Paul put on his old baseball cap and sunglasses and pulled close to the back of Bob's car. When Bob went through the intersection, Paul went through, staying really close so he wouldn't get caught at the intersection. Once they were through it, Paul backed off a little. He followed Bob for twenty minutes before he made a turn into Slater state hospital. "So this is where they're hiding the little witch," he mumbled to himself.

Bob went to the reception desk. "Can I see Candy Thompson?" he asked.

"I'm sorry. Candy Thompson is not allowed any visitors," the nurse said from behind the desk.

"Could you please give her these flowers?" he asked as he handed the bouquet of roses to the nurse.

"Tell her her father loves her very much."

"Are you her father?" the nurse asked in a stern tone.

"No, ma'am, just a delivery person," Bob said and turned and headed for the door.

. . . . .

"Brodie here," Brodie said as he answered the phone.

"Detective Brodie, a gentleman just delivered flowers for Candy Thompson and said they're from her father. Should I give them to her?" the nurse asked.

"What! What did this man look like?" Brodie asked, concerned.

"He was an older gentleman with balding hair on top, short and plump. He was well dressed," the nurse said.

"Put the flowers in a plastic bag until I get there," he instructed. Brodie hung up the phone and called Cindy. They both agreed to meet at the hospital.

Paul was parked in the lot where he could see the entrance of the hospital. He wanted to see if Trisha showed up. If she did he was ready for a showdown. A car pulled close to the entrance, and he watched as Detective Brodie climbed out. He slouched down in his seat, just as another car pulled behind Brodie's. "It's that woman, Mrs. Patterson," he mumbled to himself.

Brodie and Cindy took the elevator to the fourth floor and walked up to the receptionist's desk. Brodie pulled out his badge.

"I have the flowers right here, Detective," the nurse said as she handed Brodie the plastic bag with the flowers in it.

Cindy held out her ID to the nurse and then proceeded to ask questions. "Did this gentleman say who he was?" Cindy asked.

"I asked him, and he said he was just a delivery man," the nurse answered.

"Did he ask you to give Candy any message?" Cindy asked.

"Yes, he did. He asked me to tell Candy that her daddy loves her very much," the nurse said.

"Did you give that message to Candy?" Cindy asked.

"No, ma'am. I thought it better to talk to you first," the nurse said.

"Look at this," Brodie said as he handed Cindy the card that was attached to the flowers. "Look at the underlined part," Brodie said.

"I wonder why he underlined *girl*," Cindy said. "I think he is trying to tell her that she is still his girl, hoping to confuse her."

"Thank you," Brodie said to the nurse. "Could you please make a note that Candy Thompson is to receive no gifts of any kind unless we approve them?" he asked the nurse.

Brodie walked down the hall to Candy's room. A uniformed officer was sitting outside her door. "Officer, in case there is a screw up at the front desk, no gifts of any kind are allowed in Candy Thompson's room unless you hear from one of us. I believe her father knows where she is, so stay sharp."

"Yes sir, Detective," the uniformed officer replied.

Brodie opened the door to Candy's room. She was lying on her bed, looking up at the ceiling. "Hello, Candy," Brodie said.

Candy turned to the sound of the voice. "Hello, Detective and Mrs. Patterson," Candy replied, not taking her eyes off the roses that Brodie was holding.

"These are for you." Brodie held them out. "They're from your mother, sister, and brother," Brodie lied.

Tears formed in Candy's eyes. "How are they doing?" she asked as she inhaled the aroma of the roses.

"They are doing okay," Cindy said. "I have a message for you from Cora and Stanley," she said.

"What is it?" Candy asked, a little shocked that they would send her a message.

"They both said they love you and they don't blame you for anything. They want you to get well so you can go home," Cindy said.

'They really said that?" Candy asked shocked, Cora doesn't even like me Candy said with tears running down her cheeks.

"That's where you're wrong, sweetie," Cindy said. "Cora is very upset that I won't let you go home now. She realizes that she has not been there for you, and she is really upset."

"Could you please tell her none of this is her fault? It's all mine," Candy cried. "I destroyed my family, nobody but me." Candy cried harder.

"No, sweetie, it was Paul. He manipulated you into believing that he loved you," Cindy said, putting her arms around Candy.

"When can I see my family?" Candy cried.

"Let Detective Brodie and I talk about it in the hallway, and we will be right back in," Cindy said.

Brodie and Cindy walked down the hall so Candy couldn't hear them talk. "Paul knows she is here," Cindy said.

"What do you want to do?" Brodie asked. "She is safe here."

"I don't believe she is. Paul is very cunning. I say we send her with her family and station an officer outside the house," Cindy said.

"Are you serious?" Brodie asked. "He could be parked outside right now watching."

"I have a plan," Cindy said. "I know you're not thrilled with moving her, but it's easier to watch one place then two."

"Okay, what's your plan?" Brodie asked.

"Let's go into the room and tell Candy. This way I only have to explain it once," Cindy said.

"Candy, how do you feel about going home with your family?" Cindy asked.

Candy's face lit up. "Are you serious? Yes!" she yelled. "I want to go home," Candy said, bouncing on the bed.

"We think your father may be watching, so here is the plan. We will take you out of here by ambulance. The ambulance exit is in the basement. I'll have the officer who is sitting outside the door escort you down with a nurse, and Detective Brodie and I will meet you at your family's house."

"You're not going with me?" Candy asked in a panicked voice.

"We can't. If Paul is watching, it would be too dangerous for us to go with you. We will meet you there. Don't worry. You're safe."

Paul watched Cindy and Brodie leave the hospital. He decided to go home. It was getting late. He was tired from not sleeping while he was in prison. Just as he started to pull out, an ambulance came and almost hit him. Paul was furious as he beeped the horn and yelled at the driver.

Cindy and Brodie got to the townhouse before the ambulance. Cindy went up and gave the secret knock.

Trisha opened the door. She spotted Brodie with Cindy and turned pale. "What's going on?" she asked in a shaky voice as she held the door open for Brodie and Cindy to come in.

"Candy is on her way here," Cindy said.

"Oh my god!" Trisha said as her hand flew to her mouth.

"She will be here soon. Paul found out she was in the hospital and sent her roses," Cindy explained.

"My poor baby! She must have been devastated," Trisha said with tears running down her cheek.

"She doesn't know that Paul sent them. The hospital called us, and we went down and removed the card from the roses and told Candy the roses were from you," Brodie explained.

Trisha sat on the couch, not believing what she was hearing. She looked up at Cora and Stanley who stood quietly by. "Cora, get my purse," Trisha ordered.

Cindy sat next to Trisha. "We feel Candy will be safer here," she said as she put her hand on Trisha's. "You need to keep a close eye on her. Make sure she stays away from the windows and don't let her get to your cell phone or house phone. If she calls Paul, everything is blown," Cindy explained.

"Don't worry. I'll watch her like a hawk and so will everybody else. I want Paul in prison where he belongs," Trisha said angrily.

Cora handed her mother her purse. Trisha took thirty dollars out and handed it to Cindy, for the roses.

Cindy looked confused, "You don't have to pay for them. Paul already did."

"No," Trisha snapped. "I don't want anything from him. Since Candy thinks the roses are from us, then I want to pay for them."

Cindy took the money. "I will donate this money to the children's center for abused children," Cindy said.

Trisha smiled. "That's a great idea. Donate it in the name of my mother-in-law," Trisha said.

Cindy smiled. "I will." Just then they heard a rescue siren come on and go off, and then come on and go off again. "That's the code," Cindy said as she stood up.

"The code," Trisha said. "For what?"

"Candy, she is here," Brodie said as he peeked out the door and then went out. He was gone less than a minute and walked back in with Candy.

Trisha ran to Candy. They both clung to each other crying. "Mommy, I'm so sorry," Candy cried. "Please forgive me," she sobbed louder.

"Oh my baby," Trisha said, wiping away Candy's tears. "It's not your fault," Trisha said, looking into Candy's eyes. "You have nothing to apologize about. I love you, baby," Trisha cried.

Cora and Stanley went to join in on the hug. "Sis, I'm so sorry I wasn't nicer to you," Cora cried. "I do love you even though I never showed it," Cora continued.

Samantha, Penny, and Walter stood near the wall, giving Trisha and the kids time together.

Cindy cleared her throat, "I'm sorry to interrupt, but there are a few things we need to discuss, and then we will get out of your way."

Trisha sat down, still holding Candy's hand as Candy sat down. Cora sat next to Candy with her arm around her shoulder. Stanley stood near Samantha.

"Candy, we have a few rules you must follow if you want to stay here," Cindy said sternly looking at Candy.

"Okay," Candy said. "What are they?"

"No phone calls whatsoever," Cindy said. "And you need to stay away from the windows and not go outdoors. You will have a counselor who will come every other day, as well as tutoring with your brother, sister, and cousins," Cindy explained.

"If you break any of these rules, I will have to put you in the detention center for your own safety," Brodie added.

"I won't break any rules. I promise," Candy said. "I'm not about to put my family in any more danger."

"Then we will leave you to reunite," Cindy said as they

headed for the door. Brodie turned around and looked at them all one more time before leaving. He couldn't wait to get home with his boys. Moments like this make you realize how important family is.

As soon as Brodie got home, he took Jessica in his arms and planted a big kiss on her lips and looked around for the boys.

"What's this all about?"Jessica asked as she went back to the stove to finish dinner.

Brodie explained to her about Candy and how he realized he could lose his family anytime and that he wanted to spend as much time as possible with them.

"Don't talk like that," Jessica snapped. "It sounds as though you're dying. I understand how you feel, but to talk as if this is our last day together gives me the creeps."

"I'm sorry, baby. I just want you to know how important you and the boys are to me," Brodie said as he kissed her again. "Speaking of the boys, where are they?" Brodie asked.

"Playing down the street," Jessica said.

After the boys were fed and had had their bath, Brodie played with them until their bedtime. After they were tucked in and sound asleep, Brodie turned to Jessica. "Let's go up to bed. It's been awhile since we made love," we whispered into Jessica's ear.

Jessica giggled, "It has been awhile." The boys had come down with the chicken pox, and she had been up nights taking care of them. When they recovered, Betty Thompson was murdered. She followed Brodie into the bedroom and closed the door.

. . . . .

"Bill, I need a favor," Paul said into the phone. "You're the best P.I. there is, and I need you to find my wife for me," Paul said to his longtime friend.

Brodie was up early the next morning. He jumped into the shower and then headed downstairs for coffee. He spotted Jessica at the stove making breakfast. He went over and planted a big kiss on her lips.

"You're up early," Jessica said as she scrambled the eggs and took the toast out of the toaster.

"I need to get to the station and see if there is any news on Carman Ramosa, the little girl that's missing," Brodie said.

After breakfast Brodie gave Jessica a kiss and told the boys to behave as he left to go to the station. Brodie was at his desk no more than five minutes when the phone rang. "Brodie here."

"Detective Brodie, this is the Texas state police. We found your girl but lost track of her again."

"What? How did you find her and then lose her again?" Brodie asked.

"The guy that kidnapped her, Richard Sty, is a well known drug runner down here as well as known for kidnapping and selling little girls. Every time we get close, he disappears. He finds another woman that has a little girl or a couple of girls. He goes with her long enough to kidnap the girls," the state trooper explained.

"How does he keep getting away?" Brodie asked. "I looked into the most wanted files and could not find this guy. He has no record."

"He uses an alias. His real name is Tyrone Styles. He also has a lot of powerful friends that hide him out and help."

"Did you see the girl? And if so, is she okay?" Brodie asked.

"We didn't personally see her, but our informant did. He said she looked good. What I don't understand is why she is still with him and why he hasn't sold her yet," the trooper said.

Let's just hope he doesn't, because if he does we may never see her again," Brodie said.

"Keep me in touch," Brodie said as he hung up.

He ran Tyrone Styles through the system. His face popped up on the screen next to his picture. So did all his aliases, and next to his real name was typed A.K.A. Sty. Brodie looked at his arrest history, from armed robbery to drug trafficking. *Why is this guy still on the streets?* Brodie thought. He knew he had to call Ms. Ramosa and let her know what kind of guy Sty was.

"Oh my god," Ms. Ramosa cried. "How could I let that man anywhere near my daughter?"

"Ms. Ramosa, don't be hard on yourself. The good news is that she is still with him, and she looks good," Brodie said, trying to sound reassuring.

"Thank you, Detective. Please bring my baby home," she cried and then hung up.

Brodie sat with the receiver in his hand for a moment and then hung up.

Paul opened his door and let Bill in. "What did you find out," Paul asked as he handed Bill a drink and pointed to the couch for him to sit.

"Well for one thing, Candy is no longer in the hospital," Bill said.

"What? I was there late last night. I saw the prosecutor and detective leave. Candy was not with them, so how did they get her out?" Paul asked.

"I talked to a few friends at the hospital that owe me favors, and they claimed that Candy was smuggled out in an ambulance," Bill said, taking a long sip of his drink.

"An ambulance," Paul said, and then he remembered the ambulance that almost hit him. "She was in it. What about my wife?" he asked.

"I'm working on that. All I know is that the prosecutor and Detective Brodie are hiding them out," Bill explained.

"Follow them," Paul snapped.

"Paul, they're not stupid. If they notice a car following them, they're not going to go to wherever they're hiding your family," Bill said.

"I don't have time to play games. My trial will be coming up. I need them found now," Paul snapped.

"Give me until tonight, and I'll see what I can find out. I still have friends on the force. Maybe they will tell me something," Bill said as he put his glass down and got up to leave.

"Call me tonight," Paul said as Bill walked out of the house and headed for his car.

Trisha and Candy stayed up all night talking. Trisha realized how isolated Candy had been feeling because Cora was popular and a cheerleader and Stanley was the star quarterback. Trisha and Paul had always bragged about how many touchdowns Stanley made or about new cheers Cora did. It made Candy feel like in outsider. When she found out Paul was not her real father, it all started to make sense to her. And when she confronted Paul about it, he was so compassionate it, something Candy never felt from him, and it felt good.

Cora started teaching Candy cheers, not that Candy wanted to be a cheerleader, but it felt good to be doing something with her sister.

Paul was watching the football game when there was a knock on his door. "Bill," Paul said as he held the door open for him. "Please tell me you have something for me." Paul said.

"Yes, I do," Bill said. "But please don't ask me how I got the information," Bill said.

"I don't care how you got it as long as you did," Paul said. "So where is my family hiding?" Paul asked.

"Cindy Patterson's townhouse on the outskirts of town. It belonged to her mother. Cindy inherited it when her mother died but never stayed in it," Bill explained.

"I don't need the whole history on the prosecutor. All I want is the address," Paul snapped.

"I'm sorry. I was only letting you know that Cindy Patterson does not live there. Anyway, here is the address," Bill said as he held out the address to Paul.

Paul snatched the address from Bill, "Thanks, buddy," Paul said. "Would you like a drink?"

"No thanks. I need to get going. I have my bowling tournament tonight, and my wife will kill me if I'm late," Bill said as he left the house.

Paul sat outside the townhouse in his old Buick, watching the house. The shades were down, and the curtains were drawn shut. He could see lights on. He decided to scare them a little, just to let them know they couldn't hide from him. He slowly crossed the street and went to the back of the house and started tapping on the window.

Samantha was in the kitchen when she heard the tapping. Panic rose in her throat. She went to find Trisha, hoping to tell her without startling the kids. Trisha was sitting on the couch with Candy's head on her lap. They were watching a movie. Samantha signaled to Trisha and then put her finger on her lip and gestured for her to come into the kitchen.

"What's up?" Trisha asked as she came into the kitchen. Just then there was another tap on the window. Trisha jumped. "What do we do?" she asked.

"We need to get the kids upstairs and then call Cindy," Samantha said.

Trisha and Samantha walked into the living room and shut the TV off.

"What's going on?" Stanley asked.

Samantha put her finger to her lip and then whispered that someone was in the backyard tapping on the window and that they all needed to go upstairs.

Candy turned pale, "It's him," she cried. "He found us! Oh my god! What are we going to do?" she cried louder.

Stanley went to Candy's side. "You have to keep it down," he said. "We don't know if it's him or not. Let's go upstairs, and Mom will call Cindy," Stanley said.

They all went through the kitchen quietly while the tapping continued on the window. Once upstairs, Samantha called Cindy.

Paul couldn't understand why nobody came to the window or why he heard no voices. He should have at least heard Cora. She always freaked out at the smallest thing. He decided to head back to his car and rethink his plan.

Cindy answered her cell phone on the third ring. She heard Samantha on the other line but couldn't make out a word she was saying. "Samantha, you need to calm down. I can't hear you."

"I'm sorry, Cindy. Let me start all over. We think Paul is outside," Samantha cried.

"What!" Cindy said. "What makes you think Paul is outside?" Cindy asked, very concerned.

"There is tapping on the kitchen window. We all heard it a couple of times," Samantha said, trying to sound calm.

"I'm on my way," Cindy said. "Stay away from the windows and doors," Cindy instructed.

"We are all upstairs. We kept quiet and came upstairs," Samantha said. "Please hurry," Samantha said in a worried voice.

"Don't worry, stay where you are, and don't go downstairs. I'm on my way. I have the key so don't open the door for anyone," Cindy instructed.

Cindy called Brodie on his cell phone because she knew he would be at home. She hated to bother him, but if Paul had found out where they were, she would need back up.

"Brodie here," he said as he answered his cell phone.

"Brodie, this is Cindy. I think Paul found out where his family is," Cindy said.

"What! How?" Brodie said, as he grabbed his holster and gun.

"I'm not sure," Cindy said. "But someone is at the house tapping on the back window, and the only one I can figure who would be doing it is Paul."

"I'll meet you there," Brodie said and hung up. He explained to Jessica briefly what was going on and then kissed her and left.

Paul was very upset that no one came to the window. He decided to head home and think of his next move.

Cindy and Brodie pulled up at the same time as each other and jumped out of their cars. Brodie with his gun drawn. He pointed to the back of the house to let Cindy know he was going to check it out.

Cindy let herself in and called up the stairs to Trisha, letting her know that she was there.

Trisha came down the stairs, and Cindy could tell she was visibly shaken.

"Did you get him?" Trisha asked.

"Detective Brodie is checking the back. If he is still here, we will get him," Cindy said.

"Can we come down?" Cora yelled down the stairs.

"Yes, it's safe. You can come down," Trisha yelled up the stairs.

They all came down the stairs, Cora first, her eyes big from fright. Next came Penny and Candy holding hands. Candy was shaking and had tears running down her face. Stanley and Walter came down next. They both looked angry. Samantha came down last. She also looked shaken.

"I didn't find anyone in the back or around the side of the house," Brodie said as he came in the back door, which Cindy had unlocked for him.

"He's hiding out there somewhere," Trisha said, close to tears. "We all heard him."

"Yeah, we did," Samantha said as everyone else nodded their heads yes.

"He was out there," Stanley said. "Tapping on the window like a coward," Stanley said angrily.

"I'm not saying he wasn't out there," Brodie said. "All I'm saying is he's not out there now. I looked everywhere. He's gone."

"What are you going to do about it?" Samantha asked.

"Nothing," Cindy said. "He didn't see any of you. I think he suspects that you're here, and that's why he is tapping on the window. He is hoping one of you will look out. If we go to his house and warn him about staying away, then he will know for sure that you are here."

"We will patrol the area as much as possible," Brodie said. "Please stay away from the windows. As long as he doesn't see you, all he will have is suspicions about you being here."

SEVEN

Brodie was looking up some information on Tyrone Styles to see who his closest relatives were and if they would hide Tyrone. The computer beeped. The search was done. Brodie found Tyrone had a relative right there in Boston. Her name was Renee Styles. Brodie decided to pay her a visit.

He drove up to Renee Styles' house; it was a six-family apartment building not in the best section of town. The front door of the apartment complex was broken so Brodie just walked in and found her apartment on the second floor. He knocked twice before she came to the door.

"What do you want?" she asked as Brodie showed her his badge.

She was tall and very skinny. Her hair was black and pulled up on her head with bobby pins. She wore a pair of jeans that had holes in them and a tattered T-shirt. She had a cute face. *She could be a beautiful woman if she dressed up,* Brodie thought.

"I'm looking for Tyrone. Have you seen him or heard from him lately?" Brodie asked.

"Come in," Renee said in a tired voice. "What has my brother done now?" she asked as she went over to her daughter and washed peanut butter off her face.

Brodie smiled at the little girl, who had to be around three years old. The little girl kept saying hi to Brodie."

"Go find a clean shirt while I talk to this man," Renee instructed.

Brodie looked around the living room that he was standing in. It was very clean. The furniture was old but in good shape. He spotted a police instruction booklet on the coffee table. He picked it up.

"I will pass my test next week," Renee said

"Excuse me," Brodie said, a little confused.

"I have my finals at the police academy next week," Renee said proudly. "And then I can get my daughter and myself out of this neighborhood."

"That's great," Brodie said, meaning it. "Tyrone kidnapped a little girl, and I need to find him," Brodie said, trying not to get off the subject.

"Detective, you see my little girl. She is all I have, and I will not allow my brother in my house. I have not seen him in over a year. The last I heard he was running with some drug cartel guys," Renee said very angrily. "He is trouble always has been and always will be. He needs to be locked up for a long time."

"I agree with you. He does need to be locked up, but I need to find this little girl first," Brodie said.

"Then the rumors are true. My brother is kidnapping children and selling them," Renee said, horrified. "He is no brother of mine!" she added.

"Where did you hear that rumor from?" Brodie asked, curious.

"One of his friends was down and out. He came here

looking for a place to crash. I told him to hit the road. He then told me he had nowhere to go. I told him to go find Tyrone. And that's when he told me that Tyrone is kidnapping children and selling them and he didn't want any part of it. I thought he was just talking so he could stay here because he is not the most reliable person around," Renee said.

"What's his name, and where can I find him?" Brodie asked.

His name is Lyle St. James. You can find him on the main streets bumming money or sleeping in doorways. Everybody on the streets knows him. He won't be hard to find," Renee said.

"Thank you, Mrs. Styles, for your help," Brodie said as he walked to the door.

"It's Ms. Styles, and no problem, Detective. I hope you find him and put him away before he kidnaps any more children," Renee said.

"It's not children. It's little girls that he is kidnapping and selling as mail order brides to the highest seller overseas," Brodie explained.

"Oh my god!" Renee said as her hand flew to her mouth.

"Good luck on your finals," Brodie said. "If you need anything once you pass, don't hesitate to give me a buzz."

"Thank you, Detective. I'm glad you didn't say if you pass, because in my heart I know I'm going to pass," Renee said with a smile.

"That's why I said when you do pass. I can tell someone who is dedicated from someone who isn't," Brodie said as he walked into the hall.

"Please keep me informed with anything that goes on

with Tyrone. Not that I care about him, but I know once he is in prison a lot of parents can breathe easy," Renee said.

"I will," Brodie said. "I'll see you around the station," he said as he waved his hand and walked down the hall to the stairs.

· · · · ·

Paul knew his family was hiding in that house, and he knew what he had to do. As soon as it got dark out, he would go ahead with his plan. "They're messing with the wrong man," he muttered to himself. "If Candy thinks she is sending me to prison, she is going to be in for a big shock tonight."

Brodie called Jessica and told her he would be home late, to give the boys a kiss for him and tell them he loves them.

Brodie talked to everyone on the street, but nobody had seen Lyle in weeks. Brodie was getting ready to call it quits and go home. He was tired, and it was late.

· · · · ·

Paul walked to the back of the townhouse, looking into the windows trying to see if he could see a shadow through the curtains. When he was sure everyone was in bed, he went back to his car and pulled out the jug of gasoline. He walked to the back of the house and started pouring the gas all around the house.

Samantha heard a noise in the backyard. She peeked out the window from upstairs and saw a shadow of a man. She called Cindy on the cell phone and then went and told Trisha. Both women peeked out the window just as they saw a bright orange glow and realized Paul was setting the house on fire. They both ran to where the children were sleeping and got them up, telling them to be quiet and they needed to sneak out of the house.

Trisha called Cindy back and told her Paul had set the house on fire and they were afraid he was outside waiting.

Cindy told them to go down into the basement and out the side door where the bushes were and hide. Cindy hung up and called the fire department and then Brodie.

Brodie was five minutes from home when his cell phone rang. "Brodie here." He heard Cindy's panicked voice on the other line.

"Brodie, Paul set the townhouse on fire! Meet me there and hurry, just in case Paul is waiting outside for them to come out of the house."

Trisha and Samantha led the children through the house. The smoke was getting thick. "Get down on your knees," Samantha said. "And crawl through the smoke." Samantha led the way to the basement door.

Down in the basement, they found the side door. "We need to be very quiet, just in case he's out there waiting for us," Trisha instructed. "I'll go first and peek around." Trisha opened the side door quietly and peeked out. She didn't see anyone so she used her hand to instruct the rest to follow. One by one they all snuck out and into the bushes.

Trisha felt something hard in her back. She turned around and spotted Paul standing there, the glow of the fire shining on his face. He wore an evil grin.

"Going somewhere?" Paul asked. He held the gun to Trisha's head. "Anyone who screams or tries to run will be shot after I put a bullet through my lovely wife's head."

Everyone stood frozen. Samantha spoke first, "Paul, what are you doing? We're family. Why would you want to kill us?"

"Family," Paul snapped. "What family packs up and leaves while their husband and father is in prison, and what man then has his own stepdaughter whom he raised from a baby turn on him," Paul said as he glared at Candy, who stood close to Samantha, terrified.

"Your stepdaughter," Samantha said. "You were sleeping with her," Samantha said, not trying to get Paul angry but hoping to stall for time until Cindy and Detective Brodie got there.

Paul heard the sirens from the fire trucks, "Hurry up, let's go," he instructed as he led them to a path through the woods.

Samantha tripped and fell. When she got to her knees to stand, she realized the security guard that was hired to protect them was lying on the ground, covered in blood.

· · · · ·

Brodie pulled in behind Cindy. "Follow me," she said. "There's a side door I told them to go out."

Cindy led Brodie to the side door. It was open. Cindy then pointed to the bushes "I told them to hide in the bushes," she said. They couldn't find anyone in the bushes. "Oh God," Cindy said. "I hope they got out."

"Over here," Brodie yelled, looking down at the guard.

"Is he still alive?" Cindy asked

"Yes," Brodie said as he felt for a pulse. Brodie stood up and looked around. "Where does this path lead to?" Brodie asked, looking through the bushes where the path started.

"A playground is on the other side of the path," Cindy said. "I told them to wait here," Cindy explained.

"Maybe they didn't go of their own free will," Brodie said.

· · · · ·

"Paul," Candy said. "I only talked to the detective after he told me you blamed me for everything," Candy said, trying to sound brave as she stalled for time.

Paul stopped and looked at Candy. "They lied to you. That's what they do, and you fell for it," Paul snapped.

"I'm so sorry. I had no idea," Candy cried. "I would never have turned on you. I love you, Paul," Candy said as she cried harder.

Everyone looked at Candy, not believing what they were hearing. "Love him?" Stanley snapped. "Are you sick?" As he looked into Candy's eyes, he knew she was bluffing. He had to play along. He just hoped that Candy could see that he was playing along.

"Stanley, you don't know anything," Candy snapped back. "You don't stop loving someone that quickly. None of you understand Paul the way I do," Candy said again between tears.

Brodie and Cindy hid in the brush, listening to Candy, and could not believe what they were hearing. Brodie couldn't make a move because Paul had the gun right on Trisha's head.

"Candy," Trisha said. "Baby, do you actually believe that this man could love you?" Trisha asked between tears.

Paul shoved the gun closer to Trisha's head. "Don't listen to this jealous witch," Paul snapped.

"We can finally be together," Candy said. "It's out in the open now."

You need to tell the judge that the prosecutor and that detective tricked you into all those lies you said about me," Paul snapped.

"I will, Paul," Candy said. "Let them go, and we will go to the station together and tell them that I lied."

"Are you crazy? "Do you think I'm going to let them go before you change your story?" Paul said, annoyed.

"What are we going to do?" Candy said "We very well can't walk into police station with hostages. Do you think they will listen to you?" Candy asked.

"Shut up," Paul snapped. "I need time to think. Everyone slowly walk out of the woods and to the playground," Paul instructed.

Brodie inched closer to where Paul was, not knowing what to do, but whatever it was he had to do it fast.

Penny stood terrified when she felt something hit her leg. She turned and looked. She spotted Brodie in the bushes with his finger on his lips. She then nudged Stanley and turned her head slowly.

Stanley looked to see what Penny was looking at and spotted Brodie in the bushes. He then nudged his aunt Samantha. When Samantha spotted Brodie, she nudged Walter and Cora.

When Cora caught her mother's eye, she nudged her head in the direction of Brodie.

Now that Brodie had everyone's attention, he had to figure out what to do next, when Stanley fell to the ground moaning.

"What is wrong with you?" Paul snapped.

Stanley just groaned, and Paul walked toward Stanley. "Get up," Paul snapped. "I'm not playing games."

Stanley lay still, not moving, not groaning. He had to be totally still for his plan to work, and he hoped Brodie knew what he was doing.

Paul turned pale. "Stanley, get up," Paul snapped. Paul stood looking down at Stanley, not knowing what to do. He could hear Trisha crying.

Brodie was confused for a minute and then realized what Stanley was doing. It was Stanley's ultimate move in one of his games. Brodie had been in the stands when he saw Stanley fall to the ground and not move. When the players all stood still not moving, Stanley jumped up, grabbed the ball from the opposing team, and scored a touchdown. The opposing team could not prove that Stanley had not had the breath knocked out of him, as he claimed. He just hoped Paul didn't remember.

Paul started to bend down and feel for a pulse, when Stanley jumped up and tackled him to the ground.

Brodie came running with his gun drawn. Once he reached Paul, Stanley got off of him. Brodie would never forget the look on Paul's face.

Paul lay there stunned. He couldn't believe what had just happened. All of a sudden, he yelled for Candy. "She's ready to tell the truth," Paul snapped. "And then I'm suing you all for false arrest."

Candy went to Paul and bent down next to him. "Detective," Candy said. "Paul is right. I need to tell the truth."

Everyone gasped. They couldn't believe after all this she was still willing to defend Paul.

"Tell them, sweetie," Paul said with a grin on his face and an evil look in his eyes.

Candy put her hand on Paul's face and then pulled away and smacked him right in the mouth. "He killed my grandmother, Detective, and that's the truth," she said as she looked at Paul with hate in her eyes. "Don't ever put a gun to my mother's head again," she snapped and then spit at Paul.

Paul sat there stunned with blood running down his lip. "You piece of trash," he yelled.

"Shut up," Brodie snapped as he pulled Paul to his feet. Just then Cindy appeared with uniformed officers, who cuffed Paul and took him away.

"What happened?" Cindy said, looking around stunned.

Brodie smiled and patted Stanley on the back. "A touchdown that's what happened," Brodie said.

"What?" Cindy said.

"I'll explain it later," Brodie said. "Right now we need a place for them to stay until we're sure Paul is not getting out on bail," Brodie said.

"He is not getting out this time," Cindy said. "You can count on it."

They all walked back to the house in silence. The house was heavily damaged. Cindy stood looking at it.

"I'm sorry," Brodie said as he came up and put his arm around her shoulder.

"I have been meaning to remodel it," Cindy said. "I guess now is the time."

"Detective," Trisha said. "We have been talking, Samantha

and I, and we would like to go home to our own house. He proved he can find us if he wants."

"I think that would be a good idea," Cindy said. "He is not getting out this time. He's facing arson with seven counts of attempted murder, not counting the charges that he is already facing."

"He is looking at a very long time in prison," Brodie said.

Brodie took Samantha and her children home while Cindy took Trisha and her children home.

After Brodie dropped them off, he went home.

Brodie walked into the bedroom quietly so he wouldn't wake up Jessica. He took off his holster and locked his gun in his lockbox.

"Long night," Jessica said groggily.

"Yeah," Brodie mumbled. "Go back to sleep. I'll tell you about it in the morning," Brodie said as he sat on the bed and rubbed Jessica's leg.

"It's okay. I'm up," Jessica said. "Want me to get you anything to eat?"

"No, I'm fine. I ate in my car while I was looking for some guy who might have information on Sty," Brodie said.

"Who is Sty?" Jessica asked.

"Tyrone Styles, also known as Sty," Brodie answered. "I told you about him. He's the one who kidnapped Carman Ramosa."

"Yes, I remember," Jessica said. "You were driving around all night looking for someone?"

"Half the night," Brodie said as he laid his head on his pillow. "The other half I was at Cindy's townhouse. Paul set it on fire."

"Oh my god! Did everyone make it out okay?" Jessica asked as she laid her head on Brodie's chest.

"Yes, everyone is fine," Brodie explained the rest of the night's events to her, stroking her back as she lay cuddled on his chest.

Brodie woke up to a clash of thunder that shook the house. He looked over at the clock. It was nine o'clock in the morning. Brodie groaned and then climbed out of bed.

"Morning, sweetie," Jessica said when Brodie walked into the kitchen. "Do you want some breakfast?"

"No time," Brodie replied. "I need to get to the courthouse and see if they're going to revoke Paul's bail."

"What do you mean? It should have been automatically revoked when he was arrested last night," Jessica said, shocked.

"According to the law, he is innocent until proven guilty," Brodie said.

"But he was caught red-handed holding the family hostage. Doesn't that count for anything?" Jessica asked.

"I hope so," Brodie answered. "But he is still innocent until a jury of twelve says otherwise," Brodie said and then took a long sip of his coffee.

"Do you want some toast? You can take it with you to eat in the car," Jessica asked.

"No, I'm fine. Tell the boys I'm sorry I overslept and missed them before they went to school and that I will see them tonight."

Jessica walked Brodie to the door and gave him a kiss. "Remember you promised to spend time with us as soon as this case is over," Jessica said.

Brodie smiled. "I know, and I will as soon as this case is over." He then gave Jessica another kiss and walked out of the house.

He made it to the courthouse in record time. As he slipped into a seat at the back of the courthouse, he spotted Trisha and Samantha sitting up front with Cindy.

"All rise," the bailiff said as he stood at the front of the courtroom.

After the judge was seated, he looked down at his paperwork and then looked up at Paul. "This matter was called on an emergency basis to revoke the bail of Paul Thompson. Is the prosecutor ready to tell me why she wants Mr. Thompson's bail revoked?" the judge asked.

Cindy stood up. "Yes, Your Honor. I am ready."

"Very well," the judge said. "You may continue."

Cindy walked over to the defendant's table and then turned and looked at the judge. "Your Honor, my townhouse where the defendant's family was staying was set on fire last night, and Detective Brodie and I were called to the residence to find the defendant holding his family hostage with a gun pointed to his wife's head," Cindy said. "We believe if he remains out on bail, there could be dire consequences. Please, Your Honor, this family fears for their lives," Cindy said.

Brodie watched the judge's face. He was hard to read, but one thing for sure, he was not happy with Paul.

"Is the defense attorney ready to argue why I shouldn't revoke Mr. Thompson's bail?" the judge asked, looking at the defense table.

Paul's attorney stood up. "Yes, I am, Your Honor."

"Good enough, continue," the judge said.

"Your Honor, this is a case of being at the right place at the wrong time. My client went to the townhouse to speak to his wife. When he got there, the house was on fire. He saw a man run from the house so he went to his car to get his gun, which is registered, Your Honor. He then ran to the back of the house to see his family running through the bushes. He chased them to make sure they were okay. He was not holding the gun to his wife's head. That was fabricated, Your Honor. Please don't revoke my client's bail for worrying about his family."

"What a load of bull," Brodie said to himself. "I hope the judge could see right through this bull and see what a slime Paul is."

"I find your story hard to believe," the judge said, looking at the defense table. "For one thing if your client was worried about his family, why did he run to his car first before finding out if his family got out of the fire safely?" the judge asked.

"Your Honor," the defense attorney said as he stood up.

"Sit down, counselor," the judge ordered. "I don't want to hear from you. I want to hear from your client."

Brodie could not help but smile because he knew Paul was going to jail.

"Mr. Thompson, can you answer that question?" the judge asked.

"Your Honor," Paul said, "I saw a man run from the house. I didn't know if he was armed or not, so I got my gun just in case," Paul explained.

"You said you 'saw the guy run from the house' in your own words. Is that correct?" the judge asked.

"Yes, Your Honor, that's right. I was afraid he was armed," Paul stated.

"Mr. Thompson, you are a liar because if you did see this man run from the house then you wouldn't need your gun. The house was on fire. You didn't know if your family was trapped. You decided to run back to your car for a gun and then run to the back of the house instead of going to the front door. I hereby revoke your bail. You will remain in prison until your trial is over," the Judge ordered.

Everyone in the courtroom cheered. The judge slammed his gavel down. "Order in the courtroom. If I hear any more outbursts, I will clear this courtroom."

After everyone was settled, the judge continued. "Mr. Thompson, you will have no contact at all with any family member. That includes letters, phone calls, and relaying messages through anyone else. If you don't follow the rules, you will have an extra six months to serve after this case is done. Do I make myself clear?" the judge asked.

"Yes, Your Honor," Paul said with a scared look in his eyes.

"Court adjourned," the judge said as he banged his gavel.

Brodie waited in the hall for Cindy to come out so he could congratulate her on a job well done.

Cindy came out with Trisha and Samantha. They were both beaming with happiness.

"Well done," Brodie said to Cindy as she walked toward Brodie with a big smile on her face.

"Thank you, Brodie," Cindy said. "I didn't see you in the courtroom."

"I came just as the judge came into the courtroom so I sat

in the back," Brodie explained. "At least know you can rest," Brodie said to Trisha and Samantha.

Trisha and Samantha both smiled and then Trisha spoke, "We couldn't have made it this far without the two of you."

"Let's get out of here," Cindy said. "Besides if I know you two, you are eager to get home and tell the children, am I right?" Cindy asked.

"You sure are," Samantha said. "They are going to be relieved."

EIGHT

Cindy was sitting at her desk when her secretary informed her that a Mr. Nolan was there to see her. "Great," Cindy mumbled. "Send him in," she said as she punched the intercom button.

"Mrs. Patterson, good to see you," Mr. Nolan said as he took a seat across from Cindy's desk.

"What can I do for you, Mr. Nolan? I am very busy," Cindy said.

"Then I won't take up your time. My client Mr. Thompson wants to make a deal."

"I offered him a deal. He refused, so now we are going to trial," Cindy said, sitting up straight in her chair.

"Please just hear me out," Mr. Nolan pleaded.

"All right, but make it quick. I am very busy," Cindy said tiredly.

"Mr. Thompson is willing to plead guilty to manslaughter and statutory rape if you drop the arson charge and kidnapping charges," Mr. Nolan said as he sat back into his chair.

"First off, Mr. Nolan, your client is being charged with murder one, not manslaughter, and second I will not make any deal that will give him less than thirty years in prison," Cindy said harshly.

"My client was not in his right mind when he killed his mother. He did it out of love, and that's what I will plead to the jury," Mr. Nolan said.

"How can you sit there and say he did not deliberately kill his mother when he slowly poisoned her with rat poison for months?" Cindy asked, shocked.

"My client has no knowledge of the rat poison. He went up to check on his mother and saw her lying there in pain, crying. His heart broke for her, so he did the only humane thing he could think of. He overdosed her on morphine."

Cindy started to laugh. "Do you expect me to believe that? I'm surprised you believe it," Cindy said.

"I do believe him, and I'm sure a jury will also believe him. He is distraught over his mother's death. I'm trying to save the state money from a long dragged-out trial," Mr. Nolan said, looking a bit frustrated.

"Your client is guilty of murder one," Cindy snapped.

"Come on!" Mr. Nolan yelled. "What evidence do you have other then the testimony of a sixteen-year-old girl who is trying to save her own neck?"

"I take it you have not received my fax yet," Cindy said smugly.

"What fax? I have not been to my office yet," Mr. Nolan said, worried.

"Let's see," Cindy said as she opened her folder. His fingerprints as well as the same cologne he wears were on the tea bags. He also asked Samantha Carlton to hide the rat poison for him. The gardener will testify that Paul gave him rat poison to give to Samantha, and we have Betty Thompson's journal," Cindy said smugly.

Mr. Nolan was taken aback for a minute. "I want the journal to read before you put it in to evidence," he said.

"I have not decided if I'm going to put it into evidence or not yet," Cindy said.

"I still have a right to read it," Mr. Nolan said sternly. "Could you please give it to me?"

"Once I get it, you will get it. Right now it's with Detective Brodie, who is still investigating evidence, and as you know he does not have to hand over anything until his investigation is through.

Mr. Nolan sat back in his chair. "What if my client pleads guilty to murder and you drop all the other charges?"

Cindy looked at Mr. Nolan as though he just grew a second head. "I will not drop any of the other charges. As soon as this trial is over, he will be going to court for arson, kidnapping with a dangerous weapon, and attempted murder.

"Come on, Mrs. Patterson, can't we work out some kind of deal?" Mr. Nolan asked.

"If your client is willing to plead guilty to murder one, arson, and attempted murder I will drop the kidnapping with a dangerous weapon and statutory rape," Cindy said.

Mr. Nolan looked at her, "I'm sure we can work out a better deal than that," he said in a tired voice.

"That's my deal take it or leave it," Cindy said in a demanding voice.

Mr. Nolan stood up. "I'll talk to my client," he said in a defeated voice. "You will be hearing from me."

. . . . .

"What kind of deal is that?" Paul yelled. "Forget it! I'll go to trial before I cut that kind of deal."

"Listen, Paul," Mr. Nolan said. "I don't think your chances of getting off are good. I'm going to fight for manslaughter."

"Manslaughter," Paul snapped. "I want you to fight to keep me out of prison what I'm paying you for."

Mr. Nolan rubbed the back of his head. "Paul, listen to me. The evidence is stacked against you. If you're found guilty of murder one, you will be in prison for the rest of your life."

"And if I'm found guilty of manslaughter, I'm still going to prison," Paul snapped as he sat back in his chair with a stern look on his face.

"If you're found guilty of manslaughter, you will serve between ten to fifteen years the max," Mr. Nolan explained.

"What are my chances of getting off all together if we took it to trial and fought it?" Paul asked.

"Not good. There are piles of evidence against you, and when they get Candy on the stand to testify that you coerced her into having sex and taking part in the murder of her grandmother, that will not go over well with the jury."

"When she's on the stand, can't you prove she is saying those things to get out of going to jail?" Paul asked.

"Yes, but they will have expert testimony from her doctor at the hospital, who will state that she was indeed coerced into those acts," Mr. Nolan explained.

"So what you're telling me is my goose is cooked?" Paul said in a somber voice.

"Not exactly. If we fight for manslaughter as I said, you will get the max of ten to fifteen years. On good behavior you could be out in five to seven with time already served," Mr. Nolan said.

"Then let's go for manslaughter," Paul said, defeated.

"The prosecutor won't cut a deal for manslaughter, but we can appeal to the jury's conscience, showing how much you have done for your mother and how you hated to see her in pain. All you need is to convince one jury member that's it. The prosecution has to convince twelve."

"When will this go to trial?" Paul asked.

"We're working on that now. I'll let you know as soon as we get a set date," Mr. Nolan said. "I'm sorry, but I have another appointment I have to get to. If you need anything, call me."

Paul shook Mr. Nolan's hand and then headed back to his cell.

. . . . .

Brodie was at his desk going through some paperwork he had received on Tyrone Styles. He was last seen leaving Texas and headed toward the West Coast driving a beat up blue Chevy, and from the latest reports the little girl was still with him. Brodie put an APB out on him, and he hoped they would catch him before he sold the little girl. He needed to do more to bring this little girl home safely, but he wasn't sure what to do.

Brodie was brought out of his thoughts when the phone rang, "Brodie here," he said as he picked up the phone.

"Brodie, this is Cindy. If you're not busy, I was hoping you could come to the courthouse with me."

"Sure, what's going on?" Brodie asked.

I'm going to try to get Paul's trial pushed to the top of the criminal calendar so his family can get on with their lives."

"How does Paul's lawyer feel about that?" Brodie asked.

"He is going to meet me at the courthouse. I'll find out then. Please bring everything you have with you," Cindy pleaded.

"You can count on it. I don't want that creep loose and back on the streets," Brodie said.

"Good. Meet me there in one hour," Cindy said.

"You got it," Brodie said. After Brodie hung up the phone, he started gathering all the information he had on Paul.

Brodie pulled up to the courthouse to see Cindy outside waiting for him. He found a parking place and then went to meet Cindy.

"Do you have everything?" Cindy asked as Brodie approached her.

"I sure do," Brodie said with a smile.

When they entered the judge's chambers, Mr. Nolan was already waiting for them. He stood up and shook Brodie's hand and then Cindy's.

"Take a seat," the judge instructed. "Now that we're all here, tell me, Mrs. Patterson, why you want this case pushed to the top of the dockets?" the judge asked.

Cindy put all her and Brodie's paperwork on the desk. "Your Honor, the Thompson and Carlton families are terrified to leave their home. I want them to feel safe again, and if we can move this trial forward, it will give the family some kind of peace knowing it's almost over," Cindy explained.

"Mr. Nolan, what is your argument?" the judge asked.

"Your Honor, this is ridiculous for the family to be scared when he is behind bars."

"Ridiculous!" Cindy yelled. "He burned the house down they were staying in, and he took them hostage."

"Your Honor! He has not been found guilty on those charges yet," Mr. Nolan yelled.

"Yet, Mr. Nolan," the judge said. "Do you expect your client to be found guilty?" the judge asked with a stern voice.

"No, Your Honor, that's not what I mean. He has not been tried on those charges yet, and when he is I'm sure he will be found innocent."

"Your Honor, you have all the evidence right there in front of you, and Mr. Nolan also has the evidence. We are all set to go to trial," Cindy said in a pleading voice.

"There is one more thing, Your Honor," Brodie said as he pulled out Betty Thompson's journal and put it on the desk. "That's Mrs. Thompson's journal. If you read it, you will find out that Betty Thompson was also afraid of her son."

"Your Honor, I did not have a chance to read that journal yet," Mr. Nolan snapped.

"Are you using this journal as evidence?" the judge asked.

"I'm not sure, Your Honor," Cindy said. "I wanted you to read it first before we do because I know Mr. Nolan would object to it being brought into evidence."

"Very well," the judge said as he put the journal aside. "Mr. Nolan, have you talked to your client about going to trial and what his options are?" the judge asked.

"Yes, Your Honor. We believe there is enough evidence to prove manslaughter."

Cindy laughed, interrupting Mr. Nolan. "Manslaughter, you have got to be kidding," Cindy said.

"No, I am not kidding, and it's up to a jury to decide, not you," Mr. Nolan snapped.

"I take it, Mr. Nolan, you are well prepared to argue your case for manslaughter?" the judge asked.

"Yes, Your Honor, I am," Mr. Nolan said, looking at Cindy with a smug look on his face.

"Then I see no reason why we can't push this case forward and put an end to it," the judge said.

"What? Your Honor, I need more time," Mr. Nolan said sharply.

"Mr. Nolan, you just told me that you are ready to plead manslaughter for your client, and now you're telling me you're not ready," the Judge snapped in a stern voice.

"Your Honor," Mr. Nolan stammered. "What I was saying was I'm ready to plead manslaughter for my client, but I need more time to get my evidence and notes in order."

"I think two weeks is plenty of time," the judge said. "Trial is set for two weeks from today, and, Mrs. Patterson, I will get back to you on the journal in a few days. Mr. Nolan, I will have my secretary make a copy of the journal and have it faxed to you."

"Thank you, Your Honor," Cindy said as she stood up with a big smile on her face.

As soon as Cindy, Brodie, and Mr. Nolan reached the hall, Mr. Nolan stopped.

"You may have won this round," he said. "But the real

fight comes in the courthouse, and my client will be convicted of manslaughter," Mr. Nolan said with a smug look and then walked away.

"Manslaughter," Brodie laughed. "With all our evidence?"

"It's good to dream," said Cindy as she put her arm through Brodie's. "Let's go for coffee," she said.

"Sounds great my treat," Brodie said with a smile. "I need to talk to you about something anyway," Brodie said.

Brodie and Cindy sat in the first available booth and ordered coffee and sandwiches.

"Do you know a guy by the name of Tyrone Styles?" Brodie asked Cindy.

"I think every prosecutor around knows him. Why?" Cindy asked.

"He kidnapped this little girl name Carman Ramosa, and I can't seem to get my hands on him, nor can any other police force. The guy is real smooth," Brodie said.

"It's not that he is smooth," Cindy said as she took a sip of her coffee. "He has the drug cartel watching his back."

"So I heard," Brodie said. "He kidnaps little girls and sells them to the cartel, and they watch his back because if he gets caught then their slavery empire crumbles," Brodie said, disgusted.

"Something like that. Listen, Brodie, these are very dangerous men. I know I don't have to tell you that so please be careful and watch whose toes you step on," Cindy said.

"I'm always careful," Brodie said with a smirk.

"Brodie, I'm serious. "If these men find out that you're getting too close to Tyrone, they will gut you and then throw your body in the ocean for the sharks," Cindy said, worried.

"I know how these guys work. You don't have to worry about me. I know what I'm doing," Brodie said.

"I sure hope so," Cindy said. "I don't want to drag your body out of the ocean."

Brodie smiled. "Thanks for worrying, but I need to get home. I promised my boys I would play ball with them for a while," Brodie said as he put money on the table and headed out the door.

Mr. Nolan walked in the door as Brodie walked out. He waved to Cindy and walked over to her table. "Do you mind if I join you? I need to talk to you," Mr. Nolan asked.

"Yes, Mr. Nolan, sit down," Cindy said as she took a sip of her coffee and opened her briefcase and took out Paul's file.

"Please call me Bob." he looked down at Paul's folder. "Can we make a deal, Mrs. Patterson?" Bob asked.

"Call me Cindy, and I gave you my terms," Cindy answered.

"Please hear me out," Bob said. "My client will plead guilty to manslaughter if you drop the statutory rape and murder one charges," Bob said.

Cindy laughed "Manslaughter, he poisoned his mother slowly with rat poison. How do you get manslaughter out of that? No deal," Cindy said.

"Come on, Cindy. My client didn't poison his mother. He did give her a lethal dose of morphine to end her pain," Bob said.

"Listen, Bob I'll drop the statutory rape if he pleads guilty to murder one," Cindy said.

"What kind of deal is that?" Bob asked.

"Take it or leave it," Cindy said.

"Your husband must have trouble getting his way with you," Bob said with a smile.

"I'm not married. I know. Don't say it. I got tired of correcting people, so it was easier to let them call me Mrs. Patterson."

"Listen, I'll talk to my client, but I don't think he is going to agree to the deal," Bob said. "Are you sure there is nothing else we can work out to stop a long trial?" Bob asked.

Cindy moaned and opened Paul's folder. "Listen, Bob, your client is going to be tried for murder one. That will not change. If he pleads guilty, I will drop the statutory rape as well as kidnapping with a dangerous weapon, but that's all I will agree to," Cindy said.

Bob took a long sip of his coffee. "I'll talk to my client and get back to you," Bob said.

"I need to get going," Cindy said. "I'll see you in court, Bob," Cindy said as she grabbed her briefcase and walked out the door.

Bob tried to explain the deal to Paul. He would serve at least twenty years, and then he would be free.

"What kind of deal is that?" Paul yelled. "We're going to trial, and I don't want to hear any more about it," he continued to yell as the guard led him back to his cell.

Brodie played ball for an hour with the boys before Jessica called them in for dinner.

"How was your day?" Brodie asked Jessica as they sat at the table and picked up his fork.

"It was good," Jessica said. "How was yours?" Jessica asked.

Brodie told Jessica about Paul being held without bail

and the judge pushing the court date to the top of the criminal calendar.

"Wow, that's great," Jessica said as she took a bite of her food.

After dinner Jessica cleaned up while Brodie helped the boys with their homework. After they finished their homework, the boys watched TV for a while and then got ready for bed.

"What a day," Brodie said as he sat down on the couch, rubbing his head.

Jessica rubbed Brodie's shoulders. "You are so tense," Jessica said as she continued to rub Brodie's shoulders.

Brodie took her hand. "I'm tired. Let's go to bed," Brodie said as he got up and led Jessica to the stairs.

Brodie woke up early the next morning. After a quick shower, he went downstairs to find Jessica peeking out the window. "What's going on?" he asked.

"Probably nothing," Jessica said as she turned and smiled at Brodie. "There is a strange car that was parked outside for a while, but it just left."

"If it comes back write down the license plate number," Brodie said as he walked over to the window and peeked out.

"Here, come sit and eat," Jessica said as she pulled out his chair.

"No time. I need to get to the station," Brodie said as he took a big sip of his coffee and then put it back down. "Where are the boys?" he asked.

"They left early with some friends. They went to have breakfast at school," Jessica said. "Take some toast with you," Jessica said as she handed him a piece.

Brodie smiled. "Thank you, sweetie," he said as he gave her a kiss before he left.

·   ·   ·   ·

Brodie knocked on Tyrone's sister Renee's door and waited for Renee to open the door.

"Detective," Renee said. "What brings you back?" she asked as she held the door open for Brodie to walk in.

"I'm sorry to bother you," Brodie said as he walked in. "I just found out that Tyrone is coming back here. Did you hear anything about this?" Brodie asked.

"What?" Renee asked, shocked. "No, I have not heard a thing," Renee said as her hand went to her mouth.

"If you happen to hear from him, let me know," Brodie said as he headed for the door.

"Detective, where did you hear that from?" Renee asked.

"The other night I was looking for someone who heard from him, and one kid told me Tyrone is supposed to be coming back. I don't know if it's true or just a rumor," Brodie said.

"I promise you if I hear anything I will call you," Renee said.

"Thank you," Brodie said as he headed out the door.

Back at the station Brodie ran some more information on a few people he had found out hung with Styles. He could not figure out why he still had Carman Ramosa with him and had not sold her yet. He had to find this little girl, and he was not going to give up until he found her.

Brodie's phone rang. "Brodie here," he said as he picked up the phone.

"Brodie, it's Cindy. We have a court date set for Monday morning," Cindy said excitedly.

"That's great," Brodie said.

"Can you be ready by then?" Cindy asked.

"Well today is Friday. That gives me the weekend to be ready," Brodie said. "I will be there with bells on."

"I don't think the judge will approve of bells," Cindy laughed.

After Brodie hung up, he decided to devote that weekend to getting information on Tyrone Styles and looking for Carman Ramosa. He had to start by going back on the streets to ask questions to find out if anybody knew something.

Jessica was not happy about Brodie working the weekend, but she had known when she married him he was dedicated to his job and she had to accept it.

"Will you be home early?" Jessica asked Brodie as she packed him some food for a long night.

"I'll try to be home by midnight at the latest," he answered as he gave Jessica a kiss and hug and then talked with the boys for a few minutes before he left.

Brodie was tired. He was not getting anywhere. Nobody would give him any information on Styles. He decided to call it a night around eleven thirty. The next day he would spend time with Jessica and the boys. Maybe he would take them out to Jessica's favorite restaurant and then finish looking for some of Styles' friends.

N I N E

Brodie woke up early Monday morning. He was tired. It had been a long weekend looking for somebody who knew Styles and finding no one. He dragged himself downstairs for coffee before heading to the courthouse.

"Good morning," Jessica said as she gave Brodie a kiss. "Want some breakfast?" she asked.

"No, just coffee. I need to get to the courthouse," Brodie said as he walked over and gave both his boys a hug. "Be good for your mother," he said.

"Here, take this with you," Jessica said as she handed Brodie a muffin and then gave him a kiss.

"Thanks, sweetie. I'll see you after court," he said as he kissed Jessica again and headed out the door.

Brodie pulled into the parking lot of the courthouse and drove around for five minutes looking for a space before he found one. After he locked up his car and headed into the courthouse, he was in such a hurry that he forgot about the metal detector until he hit the door. He groaned and pulled out his badge. Once he was waved through, he went to the courtroom. He had to sit in the back of the courthouse because there were no available seats. Since it was a high priority case, Brodie was expecting the courtroom to be full. After all Betty Thompson was loved by everyone.

"All rise," the bailiff said as the judge entered the courtroom.

"Be seated," the judge said. After everyone was seated, the judge spoke. "I understand this is a high priority case, and if I have any outbursts from anyone in this courtroom, I will clear the room," the judge said in a demanding tone. "Counselors, are you ready to argue your case?" the judge asked.

Cindy stood. "Yes, Your Honor. I'm ready," she said and then sat back down.

Bob stood up next. "Yes, Your Honor," he said and sat down.

The judge gave a few more orders and then told the bailiff to bring the jury in.

"Counselor, are you ready for your first witness?" the judge asked, looking at Cindy.

"Yes, Your Honor. I call Jason Rourke to the stand," Cindy said.

Jason walked to the witness stand, and after the bailiff swore him in, he sat down and looked at Cindy, waiting for the first question.

"Mr. Rourke, what is it that you do for a living?" Cindy asked.

"I'm a forensic scientist," Jason answered.

"Could you please give us a brief history of your credentials?" Cindy asked.

"I have been a forensic scientist for ten years. During the last two years, I became head forensic," Jason explained.

"Did you investigate Betty Thompson's murder?" Cindy asked.

"Yes, I did," Jason said as he took out his notepad. "I was called around two o'clock in the afternoon to the Thompson house."

"And what did you discover when you investigated Betty Thompson's murder?" Cindy asked.

"It was made to look as if she died of morphine overdose by leaving a syringe in her arm and an empty bottle of morphine on the floor," Jason explained.

"When did you come to the conclusion she didn't die of a morphine overdose?" Cindy asked.

"I tested the tea bag that was in her cup. It came back showing that it was laced with rat poison," Jason said.

"Was it just one tea bag?" Cindy asked.

"No," Jason said. "Detective Brodie brought me three more, and they also tested positive for rat poison, as well as a small spoon and tea cup."

"Did you find anything else on the tea bags?" Cindy asked.

"Yes, one of my interns smelled cologne, so we tested it and it came back as Old Spice. We also found a fingerprint on the tea bags' labels, and it came back as Paul Thompson's fingerprint," Jason explained.

"How do you know Betty Thompson had ingested rat poison?" Cindy asked.

"I took blood work from her, and it came back that she died of rat poison. Her blood had a high content. But to make sure my findings were correct, I also conferred with the coroner, who also came to the same conclusion," Jason explained.

"Did you see anything suspicious on Betty Thompson?" Cindy asked.

"Yes, on both her arms there was bruising the size of two hands holding her down," Jason explained.

"Thank you, Mr. Rourke. I have no further questions," Cindy said.

"Counselor, would you wish to cross examine?" the judge asked, looking at Bob.

"Yes, Your Honor," Bob said as he walked over to the witness box. "Mr. Rourke, the tea bags that Detective Brodie gave you was it the same day as Mrs. Thompson's murder?" Bob asked.

"No, it was the next day," Jason said.

"The next day," Bob said. "Hmm. Did he say where he got the tea bags from?"

"I believe he said they were in the kitchen cupboard," Jason answered.

"The kitchen cupboard," Bob said. "How many people would you say were in the house and have access to the kitchen?" Bob asked.

"I have no idea," Jason answered.

"Would you say more than one?" Bob asked.

"Yes, I suppose," Jason answered.

"More than four?" Bob asked.

"Could be. I really don't know," Jason said.

"Let's move on. The cologne you found on the tea bags was Old Spice you said?"

"Yes, it was," Jason answered.

"Isn't that a popular cologne with men and women? Anyone in the house could have been wearing it," Bob asked.

"Popular with men, yes, but I'm not sure about women," Jason chuckled. "At least none that I know of."

"Anyone could have worn that cologne and have access to the tea bags in the kitchen, wouldn't you agree?" Bob asked.

Jason put his head down and answered, "Yes, I suppose so."

Bob looked at Cindy and smiled. "No further questions for this witness," Bob said as he walked back to his table.

"You may step down," the judge said to Jason. "Call your next witness," the judge said to Cindy.

Cindy stood up, "I call Detective Stan Brodie to the stand," Cindy said, looking at Brodie as he stood up.

Brodie walked to the witness stand, glaring at Paul, and then looked at Cindy as he walked to the witness stand. After the bailiff swore him in, he sat down.

"Detective Brodie, did you head up the investigation in Betty Thompson's murder?" Cindy asked.

"Yes, I did," Brodie answered.

"What did you find when you entered Betty Thompson's bedroom?" Cindy asked.

"Mrs. Thompson was lying across her bed with a syringe hanging out of her arm," Brodie answered.

"After your initial investigation, what did you find?" Cindy asked.

"I thought at first she overdosed on morphine. There was an empty bottle of morphine on the floor and a syringe hanging out of her arm, but on closer investigation I found bruises on both her arms that looked like handprints as if she was held down."

"Did you find anything else in her room that made you curious?" Cindy asked.

"Yes, I found a small spoon that had a tan substance on it.

After testing I found out it was rat poison. I also found Betty Thompson's journal," Brodie said.

"Is this the journal you're referring to?" Cindy asked as she held up the journal.

"Yes, that's Betty Thompson's journal," Brodie said.

"Would you please read the underlined portion?" Cindy asked as she opened the journal and handed it to Brodie.

Brodie took the journal and began to read. "I don't know what to do. Paul was so angry because I refused to give him money he yelled and told me I would pay then called me a piece of trash and slammed out of the house." Brodie looked up at Cindy and waited for the next question.

"Would you turn the page and read the next highlighted portion?" Cindy asked.

Brodie turned the page and began to read. "Paul is angry all the time. His temper scares me. I fear for my life, and I don't know what to do. If I tell someone and Paul finds out, well I don't know what he will do." Brodie put the book down.

"Turn to page nineteen and read the highlighted portions," Cindy instructed.

Brodie found the page and began to read again. "I hate to have these sick feelings about my own son, but I can't shake them. I asked Paul if he was having a sexual relationship with his daughter Candy, and he turned red and told me I had a sick mind and if I said a word to anyone it would be my last."

Brodie closed the book and glared at Paul.

"Detective Brodie, do you have any knowledge of Mr. Thompson and his daughter having a sexual relationship?" Cindy asked.

"Yes, I do. Candy Thompson admitted to me that she

was having a sexual relationship with her father and that they were in love," Brodie answered.

"I object." Bob stood up and yelled, "Your Honor, that's hearsay."

"Your Honor," Cindy said. "Candy Thompson is here and is going to testify that she indeed did have a sexual relationship with Paul Thompson," Cindy explained.

"Your objection is overruled. Ms. Patterson, I will let the testimony stand, but if Candy Thompson does not testify then I will throw out the detective's whole testimony. Do I make myself clear?" the judge asked.

"Yes, Your Honor," Cindy answered. "Detective, what made you suspicious of Paul Thompson?" Cindy asked.

"I wasn't at first, but after I found out he had Samantha Carlton hide rat poison for him and found Betty Thompson's journal, it just all came together," Brodie said.

"Thank you, Detective. I have no further questions at this time," Cindy said.

"Mr. Nolan, do you wish to cross examine?" the judge asked.

"Yes, Your Honor," Bob said as he stood up. "Detective, you retrieved the tea bags from Mrs. Thompson's kitchen. Is that correct?" Bob asked.

"Yes, that's correct," Brodie answered.

"Who was in the kitchen when you retrieved the tea bags in question?" Bob asked.

"The maid was," Brodie answered.

"The maid," Bob said. "Did she give you the tea bags?"

"Yes, she did," Brodie answered.

"What happened to the rest of the tea bags? And why did she only give you three?" Bob asked.

"She threw the box in the garbage. She found the three in question in the back of the food cupboard while she was cleaning it," Brodie answered.

"Hmm, she just happened to throw the whole box of tea bags in the garbage except for the three that were laced with rat poison. Do you find that suspicious?" Bob asked.

"No, I don't. Whoever laced them with rat poison is not going to take their time putting them back in the box when they can toss them to the back of the cupboard," Brodie answered.

"Didn't Mr. Thompson tell you he made his mother tea from time to time?" Bob asked.

"Yes, he did," Brodie answered.

"So wouldn't you say it wouldn't be unusual to find his fingerprints on the tea bag label?" Bob asked.

"Not if it was the tea bag he used and it was not laced with rat poison," Brodie answered.

"Couldn't someone have been wearing gloves or have handled the tea bag by the string and not leave prints? Say Mr. Thompson went to make his mother a cup of tea you would only find my client's fingerprints and not the person who wore gloves or handled the string, wouldn't you?" Bob asked.

"The only prints we would find would be your client," Brodie answered.

"Thank you, Detective," Bob said with a smile. "Didn't my client confess to having a onetime sexual encounter with his stepdaughter and that he felt so guilty that he cried?" Bob asked.

"Yes, he did," Brodie said. "But he very well was not about to tell me he had a longtime sexual relationship with his daughter," Brodie snapped.

"Your Honor, can you tell this witness that he is only to answer the question that I ask him," Bob said, annoyed.

"Detective Brodie, answer the question only. Do not give your opinion," the judge ordered. "The jury will disregard the witness's last statement."

"No further questions at this time, Your Honor," Bob said.

"You may step down," the judge told Brodie.

"Your next witness," the judge said, looking at Cindy.

"I call Samantha Carlton to the stand," Cindy said.

Samantha walked to the stand, looking very nervous. When she reached the witness box, the sheriff swore her in and then she took her seat."

"Mrs. Carlton, how do you know Paul Thompson?" Cindy asked.

"He's my brother," Samantha said.

"Could you tell us if your brother has a temper?" Cindy asked.

"Yes, he does," Samantha said. "He's had a bad temper all his life or at least as long as I can remember," Samantha answered.

"Did your parents try to get him help for his temper?" Cindy asked.

"Yes, my mother put him in counseling after he broke a boy's nose for looking at his girlfriend," Samantha said.

"What other things has he done?" Cindy asked.

"Just after he got his driver's license he wanted to take my mother's car out. It was dark out, so my mother told him no.

She didn't want him driving in the dark because he had just gotten his license. He was so mad he put his hand through a window and ended up with eighteen stitches in his arm."

"Were there other incidents that involved your brother going to the hospital?" Cindy asked.

"Yes, too many to count, but the worse time was when my mother found him and his friends drinking and she tried to ground him. He got furious and shoved her into the wall and grabbed her car keys, and when she went to grab them back, he pushed her and called her a witch and jumped in the car and peeled out. We got a call that he was in a car accident and was in serious condition. He broke his collarbone as well as his left leg, which he needed surgery on, and he had multiple cuts and bruises," Samantha explained.

"I take it the counseling didn't work?" Cindy asked.

"He only went twice and refused to go anymore. My mother tried, but my father always gave Paul his own way. He told my mother to leave the boy alone, that he would outgrow his temper. Boy, was he wrong," Samantha said sadly.

"Have you seen his temper flare more recently?" Cindy asked.

"Yes, I went to his house one day to have coffee with Trisha. Paul and Stanley were putting a go-cart together when Paul jumped up and started yelling at Stanley for putting the screw in wrong. He then took a hammer and smashed the go-cart," Samantha said.

"Let's move on to the rat poison. How did it get in your possession?" Cindy asked.

"I went to my mother's to check on her, when the gardener handed me the bag of rat poison and told me Paul had told him to give it to me," Samantha answered.

"Do you have a rodent problem?" Cindy asked.

"No," Samantha said. "That's what I didn't understand. I called Paul, and he told me that he saw a mouse and didn't want Trisha to know because she would freak out and asked if I could hang on to the bag," Samantha said.

"Thank you, Samantha. No further questions for this witness," Cindy said.

"Mr. Nolan, do you wish to cross examine?" the judge asked.

"Yes, Your Honor," he said as he walked over to Samantha. "Mrs. Carlton, you testified that your brother punched a boy in the face, breaking his nose for looking at his girlfriend. Correct?" Bob asked.

"Yes, that's correct," Samantha answered.

"In fact wasn't that boy sexually harassing your brother's girlfriend, and your brother had warned the boy time and time again?" Bob asked.

"I was not aware of that," Samantha answered.

"And isn't it true the reason he was angry and put his fist through the window is because he found out that his girlfriend's mother was in the hospital and he wanted to see her?" Bob asked.

"Yes, but my mother didn't want him driving alone at night," Samantha answered.

"When you witnessed him taking a hammer to the go-cart, didn't he tell you that Stanley had not been paying attention and he had to keep redoing his work?" Bob asked.

"Yes, but it was only a go-cart," Samantha said.

"Did you believe your brother when he told you he seen a mouse and that his wife would freak out if she saw it?" Bob asked.

"Yes, I did," Samantha said.

"Other than your children, did you have a lot of people going in and out of your house?" Bob asked.

"Yes, my kids have friends as do I," Samantha answered.

"Where did you keep the rat poison?" Bob asked.

"Under the kitchen sink," Samantha said.

"No further questions, Your Honor," Bob said as he walked back to his table.

"It's getting late. We will call it a day and pick up tomorrow morning at nine sharp," the Judge said as he banged his gavel down.

Brodie waited in the hall for Cindy. When he spotted her coming, he smiled and gave her the thumbs up sign.

"Thank you," she said as she approached Brodie and then turned to Candy. "Tomorrow I would like to put you on the stand first," Cindy said.

"Okay," Candy said. "I just want to get this over with," she replied sadly.

"I want you to follow me to my office, and we will discuss tomorrow's testimony," Cindy said.

"I will see you tomorrow," Brodie said as he headed for the elevator.

"Take care, Brodie, and tell Jessica I said hello," Cindy yelled after Brodie.

"I will," he said and then went into the elevator.

Brodie gave Jessica a kiss when he walked into the house. "So how was your day?" he asked.

Jessica kissed Brodie back and then handed him a piece of paper with a worried expression.

"What's this?" Brodie asked, confused.

"It's the license plate number," Jessica said. "He followed me to the boys' school today and then back home," Jessica said, scared.

"What!" Brodie said, alarmed. "Let me call the station and have them run this number," Brodie said as he walked over to the phone and started punching numbers in.

Jessica watched Brodie's expression while he talked on the phone change to extreme worry and then anger. He slammed the phone down and turned and looked at Jessica.

"What's going on?" Jessica asked.

Brodie ran his hand through his hair and then looked around, "Where are the boys?" he asked.

"Your mother took them out to dinner. Are you going to tell me what's going on?" Jessica asked.

"Sit down," Brodie said. After Jessica sat down, Brodie sat next to her and took her hand and held it. "Do you remember the little girl that was kidnapped, Carman Ramosa?" Brodie asked.

"Yes, I remember. Her mother's boyfriend, Tyrone something, kidnapped her," Jessica said.

"What I didn't tell you is Tyrone Styles kidnaps little girls and sells them to the drug cartel. That's who that guy was. His name is Pat Chan. He works for the drug cartel and is protecting Styles."

"I understand that Styles sells little girls to them, but why? And why would they risk protecting him?" Jessica asked.

"Because Styles sells the girls to the drug cartel for ten to fifteen thousand dollars, and the drug cartel sells the same little girls overseas for fifty to one hundred thousand dollars a very profitable income that they don't want to lose."

"Ah I see," Jessica said. "Not only are they making big money dealing drugs, they also found another way to make big money. Why are they watching me and the boys?" Jessica asked.

"Intimidation," Brodie answered. "They know I'm looking for Styles, and they want to scare me into getting off the case," Brodie said.

"Well it's working," Jessica said.

"You have nothing to be scared of. I won't let anything happen to you or the boys," Brodie said as he put his arm around Jessica's shoulder and pulled her into him.

"I want you off this case," Jessica said in a scared voice.

"What!" Brodie said, looking into Jessica's eyes. "Sweetie, I promised Mrs. Ramosa that I would bring her little girl home safely," Brodie said.

"What about your promise to us," Jessica snapped. "You promised to spend time with us as soon as you wrapped up this murder investigation."

"Listen, honey. What if this was one of our boys? Would you want the lead investigator off the case? Please, baby, I promise we will go away for a while as soon as I find Carman Ramosa," Brodie begged.

"And what about our safety? I'm scared, Stan," Jessica said in a frightened voice.

"I know you are, and I promise to get you protection. I will talk to Cindy tomorrow morning. I will protect you. I promise," Brodie said sweetly.

"Just bring that little girl home safely. I will keep you to your promise," Jessica said.

Brodie smiled and was getting ready to plant a kiss on Jessica's lips when the phone rang.

"I'll get it," Jessica said as she jumped up and answered the phone. She came back to the couch smiling as she reached for Brodie's hand and pulled him to his feet. "Your mother is keeping the kids for the night. She will drop them off at school in the morning, so tonight you are all mine," Jessica said, smiling, leading Brodie upstairs.

TEN

Brodie pulled into the courthouse parking lot and spotted Cindy immediately. He parked his car in the first available spot he saw.

Cindy spotted Brodie walking toward her. She smiled and waved. "You're here early," she said as Brodie got closer.

"I need to talk to you," Brodie said.

"Sure, let's walk and talk," Cindy said as she turned and walked toward the courthouse. "So what's on your mind?"

Brodie explained everything to Cindy. "I need protection for my family," he said as he took a breath."

"Wow," Cindy said. "I told you, Brodie, to be careful. You're dealing with some dangerous guys," Cindy said. "When do you need protection for them?" Cindy asked.

"The boys won't be out of school for a few more weeks," Brodie said as he showed his badge to the guards at the metal detector. "I'm going to lay low for a while and let them think I backed off."

"Good," Cindy said as she handed her briefcase to the guard and walked through the metal detector. "I need a few weeks to get things together so please do hang low," Cindy said.

Brodie sat in the front row of the courtroom next to Candy. He could tell she was very nervous about testifying, so he took her hand and gave it a little squeeze and then released it.

"All rise," the bailiff said as the judge entered the courtroom.

"All be seated," the judge said as he sat down. After he went over the rules again, he told the bailiff to bring the jury in.

"Are you ready for your first witness, Ms. Patterson?" the judge asked.

"Yes, Your Honor," Cindy said as she stood up and looked at Candy and gave her a reassuring smile. "I call Candy Thompson to the stand," Cindy said.

Candy got up slowly and walked to the witness stand. After the bailiff swore her in, she took a seat and looked nervously at Cindy.

"Candy, could you tell us about your relationship with your father?" Cindy asked.

Candy sat nervously in her seat, not looking once at Paul. "It was good. He was a good father," Candy said.

"When did your relationship turn into something more?" Cindy asked.

"It was after I heard my mother and Paul I mean my father arguing about him not being my father," Candy answered.

"Do you feel more comfortable calling your father Paul?" Cindy asked.

"Yes," Candy said.

"Then we will call him Paul," Cindy said. "Tell us about that argument between your mother and Paul," Cindy said.

"I was coming out of my room when I heard my mother yelling at Paul for treating me differently because I wasn't his daughter. I was stunned at first. I thought I had heard wrong, and then I heard Paul say he was not treating me any differently, that he raised me as his own." Tears welled in Candy's eyes as she stopped.

"What happened next?" Cindy asked sweetly.

"I ran to my room crying. I heard mom yell that she had to take Cora to cheerleading, so I thought I had time to myself until Paul came into my room and asked me what was wrong." Candy cried softly and wiped her tears away.

"What did you tell him?" Cindy asked.

Candy sniffled and then spoke. "I told him I had overheard him and Mom arguing and I knew that he wasn't my father," Candy replied.

"How did Paul respond to you knowing?" Cindy asked.

"He took me into his arms and cried with me, and then told me not to be mad at Mom because he was working all the time and Mom was lonely. 'She made a mistake' he said then took my chin and kissed me on the lips."

"How did that make you feel?" Cindy asked.

"I was scared and confused. Then Paul told me that he was glad that I wasn't his daughter because he was in love with me and wanted to be with me."

"How did you respond to all of this?" Cindy asked.

"I was scared but happy because all my life I felt like in outsider. Stanley is the star football player, and Cora is the captain of the cheerleading squad. I was nobody. And at that very moment Paul made me feel special, and it felt good," Candy cried.

"When did the two of you in engage in a sexual relationship?" Cindy asked.

"That night. I was scared, but Paul made me feel important," Candy said, composing herself a little better.

"Was that the only time the two of you had sex?" Cindy asked.

"No. After that we had sex a lot for four months," Candy said.

"When did things start to change?" Cindy asked.

"A month before Gram died," Candy said.

"What happened?" Cindy asked.

"He came home furious one day, saying Gram knew all about us and that we would have to do something. I asked him what he was talking about, and he pulled out a small plastic bag. I asked him what it was, and he said rat poison. He planned on giving Gram some."

"How did that make you feel?" Cindy asked.

"Scared. I told Paul he was crazy, and I didn't want any part in it. He then told me that it wouldn't kill her, it would just make her memory go a little and make it look like she was crazy and no matter what she said nobody would listen to her."

"Did you go along with his plan?" Cindy asked.

"No, not at first," Candy said. "I told him no, I wouldn't help him, and he became angry and refused to talk to me for three days."

"You must have been angry at him," Cindy said.

"More hurt then angry," Candy replied.

"When did you agree to help him?" Cindy asked.

"He came home one day all upset. He told me Gram planned on telling everyone about us so we could no longer be together. I cried and told Paul how much I love him, and he told me unless I helped him we could no longer be together. I didn't want to lose Paul. For the first time in my life, I felt like somebody," Candy cried.

"How did you help Paul?" Cindy asked, being very careful with her wording.

"Paul got some tea bags from Gram's house and would hold the tea bag up while I sprinkled rat poison all over it. Paul said that's all we had to do because he didn't want to kill her; he just wanted to give her enough so she would lose her memory. We would then put the tea bags in the wrapper and back into the box. Paul went back to grams and put the tea bags back in the cupboard because he knew that Aunt Samantha would be over to make her tea as she always did.

"Did that little bit of rat poison work?" Cindy asked.

"No, not really so Paul had another idea. He had this tiny spoon. He went to visit Gram for money and would sneak the rat poison into her tea. He always made sure he went there after Aunt Samantha because he knew she would make Gram her cup of tea," Candy explained, trying not to cry.

"Candy, I'm sorry to have to ask you this, but could you tell us what happened the day your grandmother died," Cindy asked.

Candy sniffled as tears welled up in her eyes. "Paul found me sitting near the lake and told me he needed to talk with me, so I followed him into the den. He started to cry. I asked him what was wrong, and he told me that Gram's cancer was back and she was upstairs crying and begging him to end her life.

"Did you believe him?" Cindy asked.

"Yes, I did because I had never seen him so distraught," Candy replied.

"What happened next?" Cindy asked.

"I asked him what he was going to do. He told me he didn't know, that he wanted to end her pain but couldn't do it alone, and he asked me to help him," Candy cried.

"What was your answer?" Cindy asked.

"I started to cry, so he told me to go upstairs and put the small spoon that he handed me with the rat poison on it in Gram's tea. After I put the poison in her tea, Paul came up to Gram's room. She was lying on the bed crying. She was in so much pain. I told Paul we had to call her doctor."

"And how did Paul respond to that?" Cindy asked.

"He told me he had and that's how he found out that her cancer was back, and the doctor said there was nothing more he could do for Gram," Candy cried.

"Is that when you decided to help Paul?" Cindy asked.

"Yes. I looked down at Gram, and she looked at me with a pleading look, so I knew I had to do something." Candy cried harder. It took her a few minutes to compose herself, and then she continued. "Paul told me to hold both her arms tightly while he injected morphine into her vein. He said I had to hold really tight because in her state of mind she might try to fight me. I held her arms really tight, but she never tried to fight me. Within ten minutes Gram was gone."

"Why did Paul leave the syringe in her arm?" Cindy asked.

"He wanted everyone to think that Gram overdosed," Candy explained.

"What happened after your grandmother died?" Cindy asked.

"Paul told me to sneak out and find someone to hang

with for an alibi. I looked for my cousin Penny just as the nurse screamed," Candy cried.

"Thank you, Candy. I have no further questions for this witness," Cindy said as she walked to her table, looking at the jury. They all had tears in their eyes.

"Mr. Nolan, do you wish to cross examine this witness?" the judge asked.

"Yes, I do," Bob said as he stood up and walked over to Candy. "Ms. Thompson, you testified that Paul kissed you first. Is that correct?" Bob asked.

"Yes," Candy said.

"You kissed Paul first. Isn't that correct?" Bob asked.

"No, Paul kissed me first," Candy said.

"When Paul told you he always loved you, didn't you take it the wrong way?" Bob asked.

"How could I take it the wrong way? He kissed me and said he was in love with me," Candy said.

"Didn't Paul explain to you after you took it the wrong way, even though you were not his daughter he always loved you?" Bob asked.

"No, he did not. He told me he was in love with me," Candy snapped.

"You came on to Paul, rubbing up against him and kissing him until Paul lost control and had sex with you. And when it was over, didn't Paul cry and beg you to forgive you?" Bob asked.

"I did not come on to him. He came onto me, and yes, he did cry and apologize because he said he didn't know I was still a virgin. He said if he had known he would have been more careful and the next time would be better," Candy replied.

"You came on to Paul all the time. He would have to push you away, trying to explain how wrong it was, correct?" Bob asked.

"No, that's not correct. We had a sexual relationship for four months," Candy snapped.

"If that is so, then why didn't anyone else ever see you together or suspect that something was going on?" "Bob asked.

"Because we were very careful," Candy said. "Paul made sure of it."

"Too careful, if you ask me," Bob said with a cocky grin.

"I object, Your Honor," Cindy said as she stood up. "That remark was uncalled for," Cindy snapped.

"Mr. Nolan, that remark will be stricken from the record. If you have a question, ask it, and don't let me warn you again," the judge said.

"I'm sorry, Your Honor. Ms. Thompson, you stated that you helped Paul lace the tea bags with rat poison. Is that correct?" Bob asked.

"Yes, that is correct," Candy said.

"And you helped him put the tea bags back in the box?" Bob asked.

"Yes, I did," Candy said.

"Then why is it that your fingerprints are not on the tea bags but Paul's are?" Bob asked.

"Because I didn't handle the tea bags by the label," Candy said.

"Isn't it really because you asked Paul to grab you a handful of tea bags from your grandmother's house because you loved her brand of tea. When he brought the tea home, you had him hold all the tea bags up because you said you seen a bug in one of them and you wanted him to look in all of them. Isn't that true?" Bob asked.

"No, that's not true. What I told you is the truth," Candy said.

"Let's move on to the night your grandmother died. You said Paul was crying. Did you take his tears as being real?" Bob asked.

"Yes, I did," Candy said.

"You also said your grandmother was in pain and looked at you with pleading eyes. Is that correct?" Bob asked.

"Yes, she was in a lot of pain," Candy said.

"Did you take her pleading look as a way of asking you to help end her pain?" Bob asked.

"Yes, I did," Candy cried.

"At that time did you think of you and Paul as murderers?" Bob asked.

"No, of course not," Candy said.

"Then what would you have called yourself if not murderers?" Bob asked.

"Nothing. I just wanted to end my grandmother's pain. That's all," Candy cried. "She was hurting so much."

Bob smiled. "No further questions," he said as he looked at Cindy with a smile and walked back to his seat.

"You may step down," the judge said to Candy. "Ms. Patterson, do you have any more witnesses?" the judge asked.

"Yes, Your Honor. At this time I would like to call William Sanders to the stand," Cindy said.

William Sanders walked slowly to the stand, and after he was sworn in, he took a seat and adjusted himself in his seat.

"Mr. Sanders, what do you do for a living?" Cindy asked.

"I am, or was," he said softly, "Betty Thompson's gardener for twenty years," William answered.

"So you know just about everything that goes on around Mrs. Thompson's house?" Cindy asked.

"Yes, I do. I may be getting old, but my mind is as sharp as ever," William said. "And Paul Thompson is a snake in the grass," he snapped.

"Why would you call Paul a snake?" Cindy asked.

"Because he is. That boy has no love for anyone, not his mother or family. The only time he came to see his mother was for money, and when Betty stopped giving him money, he became angry and called her names. He would leave the house ranting and raving about what a witch his mother was," William said.

"What else have you observed at Betty's house?" Cindy asked.

"I noticed Paul and Candy sneaking off together whenever the family got together. One time I followed them and saw the two of them kissing, and Paul put his hand up Candy's shirt. I was sick looking at him with his own daughter, feeling her up," William said.

"Tell us about the rat poison and how you came to give it to Samantha Carlton?" Cindy asked.

"Paul came up to me with the bag of rat poison and asked me to give it to Samantha. He said she was supposed to be here but never showed up, so I told him I would," William said.

"Did you ask him why he had the rat poison?" Cindy asked.

"No, ma'am, the less I talk to him the better. I just took it and put it aside until Mrs. Carlton came and I gave it to her."

"What was Mrs. Carlton's reaction when you gave it to her?" Cindy asked.

"She sure looked surprised. I just shrugged and walked away," William said.

"Thank you, Mr. Sanders. No further questions for this witness," Cindy said.

"Mr. Nolan, your witness," the judge said.

Bob walked over to the witness stand, "Mr. Sanders, you mentioned that Paul Thompson came over to argue with his mother. Is that correct?" Bob asked.

"Yes, that's correct," William answered.

"Did you ever witness anyone else coming over to argue with Betty Thompson?" Bob asked.

"Well yes, I believe I did," William said.

"And who might that be?" Bob asked.

"Samantha Carlton got into an argument with Betty a few times over giving Paul money. And I believe Trisha Thompson also got into an argument with Betty, but I didn't know what it was over," William said.

"So what you're saying is everybody had a chance to come over at one time or another to argue with Betty Thompson. Is that what you're saying?" Bob asked.

"Yes, sir," William answered.

"When you saw Paul and Candy together, did you have your glasses on?" Bob asked.

"No, I don't usually wear them when I'm working, but I know what I saw," William said in a bold voice.

"Wasn't Paul's hand on Candy's back supporting her because she felt faint? And what you took as a passionate kiss was Paul simply kissing his daughter on the cheek?" Bob asked.

"I know what I saw, and it wasn't a kiss on the cheek," William said.

"What color pen is this?" Bob asked, standing next to his table holding up his pen.

William squinted. "I believe it's green," he answered.

"It's blue, Mr. Sanders. You could not tell the color of this pen, but you could see Paul and his daughter in a passionate embrace farther away than where I stood?" Bob asked.

"Yes, that's true," William said.

"No further questions for this witness," Bob said.

"You may step down," the judge told William. "Ms. Patterson, do you have any more witnesses?" the judge asked.

"Yes, Your Honor. I call Trisha Thompson to the stand," Cindy said.

Trisha got up and tried not to look at Paul as she walked to the witness stand. After she was sworn in, she sat down staring straight ahead.

"Mrs. Thompson, how would you describe your marriage?" Cindy asked.

Trisha looked sad as she spoke. "I thought we had the perfect marriage. We were so happy," Trisha said.

"When did things go wrong?" Cindy asked.

"Paul started working long hours. He was determined to live the lifestyle his law buddies were living. But what Paul didn't understand was he has only been out of law school for two years and his law buddies had ten years experience. I told him to give it time and he would slowly climb the ladder. But he was insistent to do it all immediately, so he worked long hours. He was never home, and I was lonely. I had an affair and felt so guilty that I told Paul immediately."

"How did Paul take it?" Cindy asked.

"As bad as could be expected. He cursed and broke things. We didn't talk for weeks, and then I found out I was pregnant. Paul had had a vasectomy so I knew the baby wasn't his," Trisha said sadly.

"How did Paul react to the pregnancy?" Cindy asked.

"He cried and then told me he would help me raise the baby as if it were his own as long as I didn't leave him," Trisha said with tears welling up in her eyes.

"You stayed together and raised the baby. Were there any concerns about Paul treating Candy differently?" Cindy asked.

"Yes," Trisha said. "Paul couldn't do enough for her as a baby, and as she grew Paul was very strict about the way we dressed and looked. He wanted us to dress as if we had more money then we really had, except for Candy. She could dress any way she wanted to."

"Were there other instances that made you worry?" Cindy asked.

"Yes. He always brought Candy expensive jewelry that

she would never wear, and when Cora would ask for something, he would bark at her," Trisha said.

"Did you have any knowledge of your husband and daughter having an affair?" Cindy asked.

Trisha started to cry. "Yes," she said. "I was so ashamed," Trisha said as she cried harder. "I came home early one day and found them in bed together. I started yelling and screaming. Paul grabbed me by the arm and told me to shut up and if I didn't want to see Stanley and Cora hurt to keep my mouth shut." Trisha started crying harder.

"I'm sorry, Trisha. Would you like a break?" Cindy asked.

"No, I just want to get this over with." Trisha said. Trisha dabbed her eyes and then continued. "I grabbed the phone to call the cops and told Paul he would never get away with this. Paul just laughed and asked Candy, 'Were we doing anything wrong?' Candy smiled and said no. Paul told me he would have me locked up in the hospital if I said anything to anyone and that I would never see my children again. There were so many signs, but I just pushed them away, thinking Paul would never do anything to hurt our daughter." Trisha cried a little more.

"You said all the signs were there. What were they?" Cindy asked.

"They were always insisting on doing things alone. If they were in a room together, when I walked in they both would jump up. Paul told me Candy was upset about some boy and needed a man's opinion. I can't believe I missed all the signs," Trisha cried.

"No further questions," Cindy said as she walked back to her table.

"Mr. Nolan, do you have any questions for this witness?" the judge asked.

"Yes, Your Honor, I do," Bob said as he walked to the witness stand. "Mrs. Thompson, you said you had no idea that Paul and Candy were having an affair until you walked in on them. Is that correct?" Bob asked.

"Yes, that's true," Trisha said.

"Did you ever think that was because there was no affair? What you saw was the one time they were together, and Paul was crying," Bob asked.

"Candy would not make up such a thing," Trisha snapped. "Paul was not crying, and I believe Candy when she said it was going on for months."

"And how do you know that? After all you didn't have any idea of a so-called affair," Bob asked.

"Because I know my daughter, and I saw the pain and hurt in her eyes. She would never make up something so horrible," Trisha snapped.

"No further questions for this witness," Bob said as he walked back to his table.

"You may step down, Ms. Patterson. Any more witnesses?" the judge asked.

"No, Your Honor," Cindy said as she stood up.

"Very well. It's late. We will convene until tomorrow when the defense will call his first witness. Court adjourned," the judge said as he banged his gavel.

ELEVEN

Jessica woke Brodie up early the next morning. He groaned as he opened his eyes.

"The car is parked outside again," Jessica said in a scared voice.

"What!" Brodie said as he jumped up and threw his clothes on. He peeked out the window and spotted a tan Buick parked against the curb. Brodie went downstairs and headed for the back door.

"What are you going to do?" Jessica asked, scared.

"Don't worry, sweetie. Put some coffee on please," Brodie said as he went out the back door.

Jessica peeked out the window and saw Brodie sneaking up from the back of the house.

Brodie was nervous as he approached the car. Just as he got close to the front window, he reached in and grabbed the guy around the throat.

"What's going on?" the guy yelled.

"I'm going to remove my hand. I have a gun. You make one false move, and I will splatter your brains all over this car."

"What do you want?" the guy asked.

"I want you to stay away from my family. You want me to back off from Styles, fine. I'll back off," Brodie snapped.

"How do I know you're telling the truth?" the guy snapped.

"Because my family means more to me than Styles does," Brodie barked back.

"Mr. Styles will be happy to hear that," the guy said with a smile as he started his car and drove off.

"What happened?" Jessica asked as Brodie walked in the door.

"You won't have to worry about him for a while," Brodie said as he poured a coffee and sat down at the table.

"Tell me what happened," Jessica said as she put a muffin in front of Brodie.

Brodie explained everything that happened as he ate his muffin and drank his coffee. "This is nice, having a quiet cup of coffee with you," Brodie said.

Just then the boys came bouncing down the stairs.

"Spoke too soon," Jessica said, laughing as she got up to make breakfast for the boys.

After the boys were fed and dressed for school, Jessica said they could watch TV for a while.

"I need to go," Brodie said as he gave Jessica a kiss and hugged the boys. "Be good," he told them.

Brodie told Cindy what had happened with the guy at the house.

"Brodie, you are playing with fire. You do know that, don't you?" Cindy asked.

"Yeah, I know. But I need to bring this little girl home and put Styles where he belongs," Brodie said. "There's just one thing that confuses me," Brodie added.

"What's that?" Cindy asked.

"Why he still has the little girl with him. He had more than enough time to sell her," Brodie said.

"Just thank your lucky stars he hasn't or you would never get her back," Cindy said.

"Yes, I know, and I hope I get to him before he does sell her," Brodie said as they walked into the courtroom and took a seat.

"All rise," the bailiff said as the judge entered the courtroom.

"Be seated," the judge said. "I'm sure I don't need to remind you of the rules of my courtroom," the judge added.

After the jury was seated, the judge turned to Bob. "Mr. Nolan, call your first witness," the judge said.

"Yes, Your Honor," Bob said. "I call Paul Thompson to the stand."

Paul walked to the stand looking smug. He walked with confidence and poise. After he was sworn in, he sat down and adjusted his tie and sat straight up.

"Paul, did you have an affair with your stepdaughter?" Bob asked.

"Absolutely not," Paul said smugly.

"Then why do you think Candy would make up such a thing?" Bob asked.

"I think it's her way of getting back at her mother for having an affair. She was very angry when she found out that I wasn't her father," Paul stated.

"What happened the day she found out that you were not her father?" Bob asked.

"I found her crying in her room. I sat down on the bed and asked her what was wrong, and she told me she overheard her mother and I arguing and she knew I was not her father," Paul said.

"What happened next?" Bob asked.

"I held her, and she cried in my shoulder. I kissed her head and told her that I have always loved her as if she were my own daughter," Paul answered.

"How did you come to have sex with your daughter?" Bob asked.

"She started kissing my neck and rubbing up against me and telling me that she was in love with me." Paul took a deep breath and then continued. "I tried to explain to her that I was her father and the feelings she had were out of hurt and she would come to her senses after she calmed down. But she continued to kiss me and touch me, and I lost control," Paul said with tears welling up in his eyes. "I will never forgive myself for it. I tried to explain this to Candy, but she refused to listen. She insisted that we were in love, so I had to do everything I could to avoid her," Paul explained.

"Did you make a pact with Candy to poison your mother?" Bob asked.

"No!" Paul yelled. "She made that up because she is angry that I refused to be alone with her. She is very deceitful." Paul said.

"What happened the day your mother died?" Bob asked.

"I went up to check on her because she did not look good. When I got to her room, Candy was already there, holding her grandmother's hand and crying. She said that my mother was in a lot of pain and wanted Candy to end her life. I was stunned, so I sat down next to my mother. And she was in a great deal of pain, looking at me with tears in her eyes, so I knew Candy was right. My mother was asking us to end her pain," Paul cried.

"What do you do?" Bob asked.

"I walked over to the window to think. When I turned back around, I saw a syringe and a bottle of morphine on her nightstand. Without thinking I filled the syringe and told Candy to hold her arms, and I injected her with the morphine."

"Did you murder your mother, Paul?" Bob asked.

"No, I ended her pain," Paul said.

"No further questions?" Bob said, trying to keep the testimony short and sweet.

"Ms. Patterson, do you wish to cross exam?" the judge asked.

"Yes, I do," Cindy said, still a little taken back on how quickly Bob had ended Paul's testimony.

"Do you mind if I call you Paul?" Cindy asked.

"No," Paul said. "Everyone has been doing it for the last few days," he said with a smile.

"You testified that you never had a sexual relationship with your daughter. Is that correct?" Cindy asked.

"Yes, that's true," Paul said.

"Then why did you buy a Candy a pendent that said *with all my love, Paul?*" Cindy asked.

"Because she is my daughter. I wanted to let her know how much I love her," Paul said.

"Did you ever buy Cora jewelry and inscribe it the same way you inscribed Candy's?" Cindy asked.

"Well no," Paul said.

"Why not?" Cindy asked.

"Because Cora is outgoing and has tons of friends. I wanted to make Candy feel special. She doesn't have friends and is a loner," Paul tried to explain.

"So what you're saying is Cora is not special enough to give jewelry to?" Cindy asked.

"No. That's not what I'm saying," Paul snapped. "I love both my daughters."

"When you had sex with Candy, didn't you tell her you wanted to divorce Trisha and marry her?" Cindy asked.

"No! That's the craziest thing I ever heard," Paul said.

"Then why did you buy her this diamond ring?" Cindy asked as she held up a ring.

Paul looked flushed. "She said she always wanted a diamond ring, and she was doing great in school and her birthday was coming up. I decided to buy it for her," Paul explained.

"What did Cora want for her birthday?" Cindy asked.

Paul thought for a minute. "A crystal pendant," he answered.

"Did you buy it for her?" Cindy asked.

"No. It was one hundred dollars," Paul snapped.

"Oh I see. You won't buy Cora a hundred dollar pendant, but you will buy Candy a very expensive diamond ring, is that right?" Cindy asked.

"Yes, but it's not like that. Cora is very superficial and only wants it to wear for appearance. Candy wants it for memories, something she can treasure and pass down," Paul explained.

"How did you come up with the rat poison idea?" Cindy asked.

"I have no idea what you're talking about," Paul said.

"Your fingerprints were all over the tea bag labels. You expect us to believe you held them all up, inspecting them for bugs?" Cindy asked.

"Yes, I do because it's the truth," Paul said.

"Then how do you explain how the tea bags got back into your mother's cupboard?" Cindy asked.

"I don't know. I didn't put them in there," Paul answered.

"You didn't have an affair with your daughter. You didn't put rat poison in the tea bags, and you didn't put the same tea bags that have your fingerprints all over them back in the cupboard. Is that correct?" Cindy asked.

"Yes, that's correct," Paul answered.

"Everyone is lying, and all the evidence is wrong. Is that what you want the court to believe?" Cindy asked.

"Yes, I do because it's the truth," Paul said.

"When you went to check on your mother the day of her birthday, you said Candy was already in the room. Is that correct?" Cindy asked.

"Yes, that's correct" Paul said.

"Then how would you explain the maid, Natalie, saying that she was near the lake when she overheard you telling Candy you needed to talk to her?" Cindy asked.

"That was earlier in the day before I went up to check on my mother," Paul said.

"Your mother was found dead around one o'clock. You went to talk to Candy at twelve thirty. Not much of a time distance, was there?" Cindy asked.

"I only talked to Candy for two minutes, just enough time to tell her to stop following me around. Fifteen minutes later I went up to check on my mother, and Candy was already there. I assumed she went right up after I told her to leave me alone," Paul said.

"If you wanted her to leave you alone, then why would you have her help you give your mother a lethal dose of morphine?" Cindy asked.

"Because I couldn't do it alone," Paul answered.

"Wouldn't you worry about her holding it over your head?" Cindy asked.

"I wasn't thinking straight. My mind was all jumbled, worrying about my mother and the pain she was in. All I wanted to do was end her pain," Paul cried.

"No further questions, Your Honor," Cindy said as she headed for her table.

"You may step down," the judge told Paul.

The rest of the trial was very short. Bob only had two other witnesses that testified that Paul was a loving husband and father. After closing arguments the jury went into the jury room to decide Paul's fate.

Brodie stayed home the next two days, spending time with his family while he waited for the jury's verdict. He knew after two days it wasn't a good sign. He was outside playing ball with the boys when Jessica called him.

"Cindy just called. She said the jury is in," Jessica said.

Brodie kissed the boys and promised to finish the game later. He then kissed Jessica and headed to the courthouse.

"Brodie, over here," Cindy yelled when she saw Brodie in the hallway of the courthouse.

Brodie walked over to Cindy, who was standing there talking to a very nervous Trisha and Candy.

"Let's go in," Cindy said as she led the family into the courtroom. "I will be right in," she told Trisha. She hung back and grabbed Brodie's arm.

"What's up?" Brodie asked.

"If Paul walks we need to find some kind of protection for his family," Cindy said in a somber voice.

"I know," Brodie said. "Do you think he will get off?" Brodie asked.

"I don't know. Usually if the jury doesn't come right back with a guilty verdict, it's not good," Cindy answered.

"Let's go find out," Brodie said as he headed into the courtroom. He took a seat next to Trisha and held her hand as the jury entered the courtroom.

"Mr. Foreman, has the jury reached a verdict?" the judge asked.

"Yes, Your Honor, we have," the foreman answered.

"As the verdict is read, I don't want any outbursts of any kind or you will be held in contempt," the judge said loudly. "Mr. Thompson, please rise."

Everyone watched Paul stand, looking very at ease and confident.

"Mr. Foreman, please read the verdict," the judge said.

"On the count of statutory rape, we, the jury, find the defendant guilty. On the count of lewd behavior upon a child, we find the defendant guilty."

Brodie felt Trisha squeeze his hand, waiting for the final verdict. Tears were running down her and Candy's cheeks. Brodie also watched Cindy, who sat as though she was praying, something he had been doing.

"On the count of giving an illegal substance to do harm, guilty, on the count of murder one, guilty."

Everyone gave a sigh of release. Trisha grabbed Candy, and they both started crying and holding one another.

"One by one I want the jury to tell me their verdict on all counts," the judge said.

One by one they all stood and gave their verdict.

"The jury may be dismissed. After the jury left, the judge turned to Paul. "Mr. Thompson, you have been found guilty of having sex with your own stepchild, whom you raised and swore that you would love as if she were your own. I find you despicable and cowardly to use a young girl to carry out your deadly crime. You will be sentenced in two weeks. Bailiff, take him away," the judge ordered.

Brodie met Cindy and the Thompson and Carlton family in the hall. They were all crying but relieved that it was over.

Paul was sentenced to life for the murder of his mother and fifteen years for statutory rape and lewd acts upon a child.

After another long trial, Paul was found guilty of arson with intent to murder, seven counts of attempted murder and kidnapping with a dangerous weapon. He received a life sentence for every attempted murder charge and ten years for kidnapping with a dangerous weapon and ten years for arson. He would serve his time consecutively. Paul Thompson would never see the light of day.

Candy Thompson was sentenced for her act of helping Paul kill his mother. She received two years in the state hospital to undo the damage Paul did to her and five years probation.

The Thompson family sold their home and bought a new one close to the state hospital.

The Thompson and Carlton children kept their promise and donated half their money to Candy.

Brodie put his family in a safe house while he tracked down Tyrone Styles. He was determined to bring Carman Ramosa home.

VOLUME 2

Lost but Not Forgotten

Brodie is hot on Styles' case, and the drug cartel is set on finding Brodie's family. Carman Ramosa is still with Styles, but for how long? Can Brodie get to her in time before the drug cartel finds his family? Read Volume 2.

listen|imagine|view|experience

AUDIO BOOK DOWNLOAD INCLUDED WITH THIS BOOK!

In your hands you hold a complete digital entertainment package. Besides purchasing the paper version of this book, this book includes a free download of the audio version of this book. Simply use the code listed below when visiting our website. Once downloaded to your computer, you can listen to the book through your computer's speakers, burn it to an audio CD or save the file to your portable music device (such as Apple's popular iPod) and listen on the go!

How to get your free audio book digital download:

1. Visit www.tatepublishing.com and click on the e|LIVE logo on the home page.
2. Enter the following coupon code:
   8322-1a41-c27d-c5f7-c677-6de3-e2c5-aabb
3. Download the audio book from your e|LIVE digital locker and begin enjoying your new digital entertainment package today!